IN THE CAFÉ
OF LOST YOUTH

Also by Patrick Modiano in English translation

PATRICK MODIANO

IN THE CAFÉ
OF LOST YOUTH

Translated from the French by
Euan Cameron

MACLEHOSE PRESS
QUERCUS · LONDON

First published in the French language as *Dans le café de la jeunesse perdue* by
Editions Gallimard, Paris, in 2007
First published in Great Britain in 2016 by

MacLehose Press
An imprint of Quercus Publishing Ltd
Carmelite House
50 Victoria Embankment
London EC4Y 0DZ

An Hachette UK company

A CIP catalogue record for this book is available
from the British Library.

ISBN (HB) 978 0 85705 526 2
ISBN (Ebook) 978 0 85705 527 9

10 9 8 7 6 5 4 3 2 1

Designed and typeset in Albertina by Libanus Press, Marlborough
Printed and bound in Great Britain by Clays Ltd, St Ives plc

Halfway along the path of real life,
we were encircled by a dark melancholy,
expressed by so many sad and mocking words,
in the café of lost youth.

GUY DEBORD

OF THE TWO ENTRANCES TO THE CAFÉ, SHE ALWAYS used the narrower one, the one they called the shady door. She chose the same table to the rear of the small room. To begin with, she did not speak to anyone, then she got to know the regulars of Le Condé, most of whom were our age, I would say between nineteen and twenty-five years old. She would sometimes sit down at their tables, but, more often, she stuck to her spot, right at the back.

She did not come at any regular time. You might find her sitting there very early in the morning. Or else she would appear at about midnight and stay until closing time. Together with Le Bouquet and La Pergola, it was one of the cafés that closed latest in the neighbourhood, and it was the one with the oddest clientele. I wonder, over time, whether it was not her presence alone that gave this place and these people their oddness, as though she had permeated them all with her aroma.

Supposing that you had been blindfolded and transported there, that you had been placed at a table, your blindfold removed and that you had been given a few minutes to answer the question: What part of Paris are you in? It would have been enough for you to observe your neighbours and listen to their comments and you would perhaps have guessed: in the vicinity of the carrefour de l'Odéon, which I imagine to be still as gloomy when it rains.

A photographer had walked into Le Condé one day. Nothing in his appearance set him apart from the customers. The same age, the same scruffy clothing. He wore a coat that was too long for him, cotton trousers and large military boots. He had taken a great many photographs of those who used to patronise Le Condé. He, too, had become a regular and, for the others, it was as though he were taking family photographs. Much later, they appeared in a photographic book devoted to Paris with just the first or surnames of the customers as captions. And she features in several of these photographs. She caught the light better than the others, as they say in the cinema. Of all of them, she is the one you notice first. At the foot of the page, among the captions, she is mentioned under the name "Louki". "From left to right: Zacharias, Louki, Tarzan, Jean-Michel, Fred and Ali Cherif . . ." "In the foreground, sitting at the bar: Louki. Behind her, Annet, Don Carlos, Mireille, Adamov and Doctor Vala." She is sitting very upright, whereas the others have relaxed poses, the one known as Fred, for example, has fallen asleep with his head resting on the imitation leather bench and he has evidently not shaved for several days. The following should be made clear: she was given the name Louki from the moment she first came to Le Condé. I was there one evening when she came in at about midnight and when only Tarzan, Fred, Zacharias and Mireille, sitting at the same table, were still there. It was Tarzan who called out: "Hey, there's Louki . . ." She seemed frightened at first, and then she smiled. Zacharias stood up and, in a tone of mock solemnity announced: "Tonight, I am christening you. From now on, you will be known as Louki." And as time passed and each one of them called her Louki, I really think she felt relieved to have this new name. Yes, relieved. In fact, the more I think about it, the more I revert to my initial impression: she was seeking refuge here, at Le Condé, as though she wanted to run away from something, to escape from a danger. This notion struck me when I saw her alone, right at the back, in this place where no-one could notice her. And when she mingled with the others, she did not attract attention either. She remained silent and reserved and was happy just to listen. And it even occurred to me that to be safer still she preferred noisy groups, the "loud-mouths", otherwise she would not almost always have sat at the table with Zacharias, Jean-Michel, Fred, Tarzan and La Houpa ... With them, she melted into the background, she was merely an anonymous extra, one of those referred to in photographic captions as, "Unidentified person" or, more simply, "X". Yes, in the early days, at Le Condé, I never saw her in private conversation with anyone. And then, it did not matter in the least that one of these loudmouths should call her Louki in front of everyone since it was not her real name.

Yet, when you considered her carefully, you noticed certain details that distinguished her from the others. The care that she took over her sartorial appearance was unusual among the customers of Le Condé. One evening, at Tarzan, Ali Cherif and La Houpa's table, she lit a cigarette and I was struck by the delicacy of her hands. And especially, her gleaming nails. They were painted with colourless varnish. This detail may seem trifling. So let us be more serious. To do so we need to provide a little information about the regulars at Le Condé. They were aged between nineteen and twenty-five, apart from a few customers such as Babilée, Adamov and Dr Vala who were edging gradually towards their fifties, though we forgot their age. Babilée, Adamov and Dr Vala were loyal to their youthfulness, to what one might refer to by the fine, melodious and old-fashioned word "bohemian". I look up "bohemian" in the dictionary: Someone who leads a wandering life, without rules or worries about the next day. That is a definition that certainly applied to those who were regulars at Le Condé. Some of them, such as Tarzan, Jean-Michel and Fred, claimed to have been involved with the police on a number of occasions since their teenage years, and La Houpa, at the age of sixteen, had escaped from the Bon-Pasteur remand home. But we were on the Left Bank and the majority of them lived under the protection of literature and the arts. I, myself, was studying. I did not dare tell them this and I was not really part of their group.

I had definitely sensed that she was different to the others. Where had she come from before she had been given her name? Those who frequented Le Condé would often be carrying a book, its cover stained with wine, which they would lay casually on the table. *Les Chants de Maldoror. Les Illuminations. Les Barricades mystérieuses.* But she, to begin with, was always empty-handed.

Then, she probably wanted to be like the others, and one day, at Le Condé, I caught her on her own, reading. From then on, her book never left her. She would place it prominently on the table, whenever she happened to be in the company of Adamov and the others, as though this book were her passport or a residence permit that legitimised her presence among them. But no-one took any notice of it, not Adamov, nor Babilée, nor Tarzan, nor La Houpa. It was a paperback, with a grubby cover, the kind you buy second-hand along the banks of the Seine, and its title was printed in large red letters: *Lost Horizon*. At the time, it did not mean anything to me. I should have asked what the book was about, but I foolishly told myself that *Lost Horizon* was merely an accessory for her and that she was pretending to read it so as to comply with the clientele of Le Condé. A passer-by who happened to cast a hurried glance at this clientele from outside – and even pressed his head to the window for a moment – would simply have taken them for student customers. But he would soon have changed his mind when he noticed the amount of alcohol being drunk at Tarzan, Mireille, Fred and La Houpa's table. In the peaceful cafés of the Latin Quarter, they would never have drunk like that. In the slack hours of the after-noon, of course, Le Condé could be deceptive. But as evening approached, it became once more the meeting place of what a romantic philosopher called "the lost youth". Why this café rather than any other? Because of the owner, a Mme Chadly, who did not appear to be surprised by anything and even displayed a certain indulgence towards her customers. Many years later, when the streets of the neighbourhood offered nothing but the windows of luxury boutiques and a leather-goods shop stood on the site of Le Condé, I came across Mme Chadly on the other bank of the Seine, on the way up rue Blanche. She did not recognise me immediately. We walked side by side for a long while, talking about Le Condé. Her husband, an Algerian, had bought the business after the war. She remembered all of our names. She often wondered what had become of us, but she had few illusions. She had known from the start that things would turn out very badly for us. Lost dogs, she told me. And at the moment we said goodbye to one another outside the chemist's on place Blanche, she confessed to me, looking me straight in the eye: "Personally, the one I liked most was Louki."

When she was at Tarzan, Fred and La Houpa's table, did she drink as much as them or did she just pretend to, so as not to annoy them? In any case, with her upright posture, her slow and graceful movements, and her almost imperceptible smile, she controlled her drinking really well. At the bar, it was easier to cheat. You took the opportunity of a moment's inattentiveness among your drunken friends to empty your glass down the sink. But there, at one of Le Condé's tables, it was more difficult. They forced you to join in their binges. They were extremely touchy about this and they reckoned you to be unworthy of their group if you did not accompany them right to the end of what they called their "trips". As for other toxic substances, I was led to believe, without being quite sure, that Louki used them, along with certain members of the group. Nothing in her expression or her manner, however, allowed one to suppose that she visited any drug-induced paradise.

I often wondered whether one of her acquaintances had spoken to her about Le Condé before she went there for the first time. Or whether someone had arranged to meet her at this café and not turned up. She would then have sat there, day after day, night after night, at her table, hoping to meet him at this place that was the one point of reference between her and this stranger. No other means of getting in touch with him. No address. Nor any phone number. Just a first name. But perhaps she had wound up there by chance, like me. She happened to be in the area and she needed to shelter from the rain. I have always thought that certain places are magnets and that you are drawn to them if you walk about in their vicinity. And it happens imperceptibly, without you even suspecting. All that is needed is a street on a slope, a sunny pavement, or else a pavement in the shade. Or else a downpour. And this leads you there, to the exact point where you were meant to end up. It seems to me that Le Condé, on account of its location, had this magnetic power and that if you were to calculate the probabilities, the result would have confirmed it: within a fairly wide radius, it was inevitable you would be diverted towards it. I know about these things.

One of the members of the group, Bowing, the one we used to call "the Captain", had become involved in an initiative the others approved of. For close on three years, he had noted down the names of the customers at Le Condé as and when they arrived, recording the date and precise hour each time. He had entrusted two of his friends with the same task at Le Bouquet and at La Pergola, both of which stayed open all night. Unfortunately, in these two cafés, customers did not always want to give their names. Basically, Bowing was trying to rescue from oblivion the moths that flutter around a light for a few moments. He dreamt, he would say, of a vast register in which the names of the customers of all the cafés in Paris over the past hundred years had been collected, with a note of their successive arrivals and departures. He was haunted by what he called "the fixed spots".

In this uninterrupted stream of women, men, children and dogs that pass by and are eventually lost along the streets, one would like, from time to time, to retain a face. Yes, according to Bowing, amid the tumult of large cities one had to find a few fixed spots. Before he left to go abroad, he had given me the notebook in which the customers of Le Condé are listed, day by day, over three years. She only appears under her assumed name, Louki, and she is mentioned for the first time one 23rd of January. The winter that year was particularly severe, and some of us did not leave Le Condé all day so as to keep out of the cold. The Captain also kept a note of our addresses so that it was possible to visualise the regular route that each of us took to come to Le Condé. For Bowing, it was yet another way of establishing fixed spots. He does not mention her address straight away. It is only on a certain 18 March that we read: "2.00 p.m. Louki, 16 rue Fermat, 14th arrondissement." But on 5 September of the same year, she changed address: "11.40 p.m. Louki, 8 rue Cels, 14th arrondissement." I imagine that Bowing used to mark out our journeys to Le Condé on large maps of Paris, and that for this the Captain would use ballpoints with different coloured inks. Perhaps he wanted to know whether we might have a chance of bumping into one another even before arriving at the destination.

As it happens, I remember having met Louki one day in a neighbourhood I was unfamiliar with and where I had been calling on a distant cousin of my parents. Having left his home, I was walking towards the Porte-Maillot métro station and we bumped into one another at the far end of avenue de la Grande-Armée. I stared at her and she, too, looked at me anxiously, as though I had caught her in an embarrassing situation. I held out my hand: "We've seen each other before, at Le Condé," I said to her, and this café suddenly seemed to me to be at the other end of the world. She smiled awkwardly. "Yes, of course . . . at Le Condé . . ." It was shortly after she had made her first appearance there. She had not yet mixed with the others and Zacharias had not yet christened her Louki. "Weird café, eh, Le Condé . . ." She nodded in agreement. We walked a little way together and she told me that she lived around here, but that she did not like this neighbourhood at all. It's ridiculous, but I could have discovered her real name that day. Then we said goodbye to one another at Porte Maillot, in front of the entrance to the métro, and I watched her as she set off in the direction of Neuilly and the Bois de Boulogne, walking more and more slowly, as if to allow someone the opportunity of detaining her. I imagined that she would not come back to Le Condé anymore and that I would never hear from her again. She would disappear into what Bowing called "the anonymity of the big city", which he claimed to be fighting by filling the pages of his notebook with names. A 190-page, Clairefontaine notebook with red laminated covers. To be honest, it does not further matters. If you leaf through the notebook, apart from some elusive names and addresses, you learn nothing about all these people or about me. No doubt the Captain reckoned that it was already something to have named us and "fixed" us somewhere. As for the rest . . . At the Condé, we never asked one another questions about our origins. We were too young, we had no past to reveal, we lived in the present. Even the older customers, Adamov, Babilée or Dr Vala, never made any reference to their past. They were happy merely to be there, among us. It is only now, after all this time, that I have one regret: I would have liked Bowing to have been more precise in his notebook, and for him to have devoted a brief biographical note to each person. Did he really believe that a name and an address would be enough, later on, to find the thread of a life? And especially a simple first name which is not the real one? "Louki. Monday 12 February, 11.00 p.m." "Louki. 28 April, 2.00 p.m." He also indicated the positions the customers occupied around the tables each day. Sometimes, there is not even a surname or a first name. On three occasions, in the month of June that year, he noted: "Louki, with the dark-haired man in the suede jacket." He did not ask this person his name, or else the man refused to answer. It appears that the guy was not a regular customer. The dark-haired man in the suede jacket was lost forever in the streets of Paris, and Bowing was unable to pin down his shadow for a few seconds. And then there are inaccuracies in his notebook. I eventually established some reference points that bear out my notion that she did not come to Le Condé for the first time in January as Bowing leads one to believe. I have a memory of her well before that date. The Captain only mentioned her from the moment the others had christened her Louki, and I suppose that until then he had not noticed her presence. She did not even have the right to a vague note such as "2.00 p.m. A dark-haired woman with green eyes", unlike the dark-haired man in the suede jacket.

It was in October of the previous year that she made her

appearance. I discovered a reference point in the Captain's notebook: "15 October. 9.00 p.m. Zacharias' birthday. At his table: Annet, Don Carlos, Mireille, La Houpa, Fred, Adamov." I remember it perfectly. She was at their table. Why did Bowing not have the curiosity to ask her name? The evidence is precarious and contradictory, but I am certain of her presence that evening. Everything that had made her invisible in Bowing's eyes had impressed me. Her shyness, her slow movements, her smile, and above all her silence. She was sitting next to Adamov. Perhaps it was because of him that she had come to Le Condé. I had often come across Adamov in the vicinity of the Odéon, and further away in the Saint-Julien-le-Pauvre neighbourhood. On each occasion, he was walking with his hand resting on a girl's shoulder. A blind man allowing himself to be guided. And yet, with his tragic dog expression, he appeared to be observing everything. And every time, it seemed to me, it was a different girl who acted as his guide. Or as his nurse. Why not her? Well, as it happened, she left Le Condé that evening with Adamov. I watched them set off down the deserted street towards the Odéon, Adamov with his hand on her shoulder and walking at his mechanical pace. It was as though she was frightened of going too quickly, and sometimes she stopped for a moment, as if to let him catch his breath. At the carrefour de l'Odéon, Adamov shook her hand rather formally, then she was swallowed up as she entered the métro. He continued at his sleepwalker's pace straight on towards Saint-André-des-Arts. And she? Yes, she began coming to Le Condé in the autumn. And that was probably not by chance. For me, the autumn has never been a sad season. The dead leaves and the increasingly shorter days have never suggested the end of anything, but rather an expectation of the future. In Paris, there is electricity in the air on October evenings at nightfall. Even when it is raining. I do not feel low at that hour of the day, nor do I have the sense of time flying by. I have the impression that everything is possible. The year begins in the month of October. It is the start of the academic year and I believe it is the time for making plans. So, if she came to Le Condé in October, it was because she had made a break with a whole area of her life and she wanted what is called in novels "a fresh start". What is more, there is evidence that I am not mistaken. At Le Condé, she was given a new name. And that day, Zacharias even spoke of its being a christening. A second birth, as it were.

As for the dark-haired man in the suede jacket, unfortunately he does not feature on the photographs taken at Le

Condé. It's a pity. We often manage to identify someone by means of a photograph. You print it in a newspaper and appeal for a witness. Was it a member of the group whom Bowing did not know and whose name he was too lazy to record?

Yesterday evening, I went carefully through every page of the notebook. "Louki with the dark-haired man in the suede jacket." And I noticed, to my great surprise, that it was not just in June that the Captain mentioned this stranger. At the foot of a page, he had hurriedly scribbled: "24 May. Louki with the dark-haired man in the suede jacket." And we find the same caption on two occasions in April. I had asked Bowing why, every time she was concerned, he had underlined her name in blue pencil, as if to distinguish her from the others. No, it wasn't he who had done this. One day when he was standing at the bar and was jotting down the names of the customers present in the room, a man standing beside him had interrupted him in his task: a fellow of about forty who knew Dr Vala. He spoke in a soft voice and smoked Virginia cigarettes. Bowing had felt at ease and told him a little about what he called his Visitors' Book. The man had appeared interested. He was an "art book publisher". Yes indeed, he knew the person who had taken photographs at Le Condé sometime previously. He was intending to publish a book on the subject, the title of which would be *Un café à Paris*. Would he be so kind as to lend him his notebook, which might help him to choose captions for the photographs, until the following morning? The next day, he had returned the notebook to Bowing and he had never been seen at Le Condé again. The Captain had been surprised that the name Louki had been underlined in blue pencil each time. He had intended to find out a bit more about this art book publisher by putting some questions to Dr Vala. Vala had been amazed. "Ah, he told you he was an art book publisher?" He knew him only very slightly, from having often come across him in rue Saint-Benoît at La Malène or at the Montana's bar, where he had even played the 421 dice game with him on several occasions. This fellow had been around the neighbourhood for a long time. His name? Caisley. Vala seemed a bit embarrassed to be talking about him. And when Bowing had referred to his notebook and to the blue pencil marks underlining the name Louki, an anxious expression came over the doctor's face. It had been very fleeting. Then he had smiled: "He must be interested in the girl . . . She is so pretty . . . But what an odd idea to fill your notebook with all these names . . . You amuse me, you and your group and your pataphysical experiences . . ." He was confusing everything, pataphysics, *lettrisme*, automatic writing, *métagraphies* and all the experiments conducted by the most literary customers of Le Condé, like Bowing, Jean-Michel, Fred, Babilée, Larronde or Adamov. "And then it's dangerous to do that", Dr Vala had added in a solemn tone. "Your notebook, it's a bit like a police register or a police station daybook. It's as though we had all been rounded up . . ."

Bowing had protested by trying to explain his theory of fixed spots, but from that day on the Captain had the impression that Vala mistrusted him and that he even tried to avoid him.

This Caisley had not simply underlined the name Louki. Every time "the dark-haired man in the suede jacket" was mentioned, there were two blue lines in the notebook. All this had greatly troubled Bowing and he had prowled around rue Saint-Benoît over the days that followed in the hope of coming across this so-called art book publisher, at La Malène or the Montana, and asking him for some explanations. He never found him. Sometime later he himself had had to leave France and he had bequeathed me the notebook, as though he wanted me to carry on his research. But it is too late now. And then if this entire period is very much alive in my memory at times, it is because of questions that remain unanswered.

At low moments of the day, on coming back from the office, and often in the solitude of Sunday evenings, one detail comes back to me. Very attentively, I try to gather together some others and to jot them down at the back of Bowing's notebook on the pages that are still blank. I, too, set off in search of fixed spots. It serves as a pastime, just as others do crosswords or play patience. The names and dates in Bowing's notebook are very helpful; they remind me from time to time of a precise fact, a rainy afternoon or a sunny one. I have always been very aware of the seasons. One evening, Louki walked into Le Condé, her hair soaked because of a downpour or rather because of those endless November or early spring rains. Mme Chadly was standing behind the bar that day. She went up to the first floor, into her tiny flat, to look for a bath towel. As the notebook indicates, gathered around the same table that evening were Zacharias, Annet, Don Carlos, Mireille, La Houpa, Fred and Maurice Raphaël. Zacharias took the towel and rubbed Louki's hair with it, before knotting it into a turban around her head. She sat down at their table, they made her drink a hot toddy, and she stayed there very late with them, the turban on her head. When we left Le Condé, at about two o'clock in the morning, it was still raining. We stood in the entrance porch, Louki still wearing her turban. Mme Chadly had switched off the lights in the main room and had gone up to bed. She opened her window on the landing and suggested we come up to her flat so that we could shelter. But Maurice Raphaël said to her, very gallantly: "Don't even think of it, madame . . . We must let you get some sleep." He was a good-looking dark-haired man, older than us, a frequent customer at Le Condé, whom Zacharias called "the Jaguar" owing to the way he walked and his cat-like movements. Like Adamov and Larronde, he had published several books, but we never talked about them. An air of mystery hovered over this man and we even thought he had connections with the Milieu. The rain intensified, a monsoon rain, but it did not matter to the others since they lived in the neighbourhood. Soon, there were only Louki, Maurice Raphaël and me in the porch. "I could drive you home?" Maurice Raphaël suggested. We dashed through the rain, down to the end of the road, where his car, an old black Ford, was parked. Louki sat beside him, and I sat on the back seat. "Who's to be dropped off first?" asked Maurice Raphaël. Louki told him what her street was, pointing out that it was beyond the Montparnasse cemetery. "So, you live in limbo," he said. And I don't believe either of us understood what "limbo" meant. I asked him to drop me well beyond the gates of the Luxembourg, on the corner of rue du Val-de-Grâce. I did not want him to know exactly where I lived for fear that he might ask me questions.

I shook hands with Louki and with Maurice Raphaël, reminding myself that neither of them knew my name. I was a very unobtrusive customer at Le Condé and I kept myself slightly apart, happy just to listen to them all. And that was enough for me. I felt comfortable with them. Le Condé was a refuge for me from all the dullness that I expected from life. There would be a part of me – the better part – that I would be obliged, one day, to leave there.

"You're wise to live in the Val-de-Grâce neighbourhood," Maurice Raphaël said to me.

He smiled at me and his smile seemed to me to express both kindness and irony.

"See you soon," Louki said to me.

I got out of the car and waited for it to disappear, down towards Port-Royal, and retrace its route. In actual fact, I did not exactly live in the Val-de-Grâce neighbourhood, but a little lower down in a building on 85 boulevard Saint-Michel, where, miraculously, I had found a room as soon as I arrived in Paris.

From the window, I could see the black frontage of my college. That night, I could hardly keep my eyes off this grandiose façade and the great stone staircase up to the entrance. What would they think if they discovered that I walked up that staircase every day and that I was a student at the École Supérieure des Mines? Did Zacharias, La Houpa, Ali Cherif or Don Carlos actually know what the École des Mines was? I had to keep my secret or else they were likely to make fun of me or distrust me. What did the École des Mines mean to Adamov, Larronde or Maurice Raphaël? Nothing, probably. They would advise me not to have anything to do with the place anymore. If I spent a great deal of time at Le Condé, it was because I wanted to be given such advice, once and for all. Louki and Maurice Raphaël must have already reached the other side of Montparnasse cemetery, in that area he called "limbo". And as for me, I stood standing there in the darkness, at the window, contemplating the blackened façade. It looked rather like a disused railway station in a provincial town. On the walls of the adjacent building, I had noticed traces of bullets, as though someone had been shot there. I repeated to myself in a low voice those four words that seemed to me increasingly strange: École Supérieure des Mines.

I WAS FORTUNATE THAT THIS YOUNG MAN SHOULD have been the person sitting next to me at the table at Le Condé and that we engaged in conversation so naturally. It was the first time I had come to this establishment and I was old enough to be his father. The notebook in which he listed, day after day, night after night, the customers at Le Condé over three years made my task easier. I regret having concealed from him the precise reason why I wanted to consult this document that he was kind enough to lend me. But did I lie to him when I told him that I was an art book publisher?

I was well aware that he believed me. That is the advantage of being twenty years older than others: they know nothing about your past. And even if they ask you a few absent-minded questions about what your life had been like until then, you can invent it all. A new life. They won't go and check it out. As you relate this imaginary life, great gusts of fresh air blow through the enclosed space in which you had been suffocating for a long time. A window suddenly opens, the shutters bang in the sea breeze. Once more, you have the future before you.

Art book publisher. That came to me without my thinking about it. Had anyone asked me, more than twenty years ago, what I wanted to become, I would have mumbled: art book publisher. Well, that's what I said today. Nothing has changed. All those years are irrelevant.

Except that I have not made an entirely clean sweep of the past. Certain witnesses remain, certain survivors among those who were our contemporaries. One evening, at the Montana, I asked Dr Vala his date of birth. We were born in the same year. And I reminded him that we had met long ago, in this same bar, when the neighbourhood still shone with all its sparkle. And furthermore, I thought I had come across him well before, in other parts of Paris, on the Right Bank. I was even certain of this. In a terse voice, Vala had ordered a small bottle of Vittel, interrupting me just as there was a chance that I might recall unpleasant memories. I said nothing. We live at the mercy of certain silences. We know a good deal about one another. So we try to avoid each other. The best thing, of course, is to lose touch for good.

What an odd coincidence . . . I bumped into Vala this afternoon when, for the first time, I walked through the doorway of Le Condé. He was sitting at a table at the back with two or three young people. He glanced at me with the worried expression of the bon viveur in the presence of a ghost. I smiled at him. I shook hands with him without saying anything. I sensed that the slightest word from me might make him ill at ease in the presence of his new friends. He appeared relieved by my silence and by my tactfulness when I went to sit on the imitation leather bench at the far end of the room. From there, I was able to observe him without our eyes meeting. He spoke to them in a low voice, leaning towards them. Was he afraid I might overhear his remarks? Then, to pass the time, I imagined all the things I might have said to him in an artificially social voice that would have brought out beads of sweat on his forehead. "Are you still a doctor?" And after pausing for a while: "Tell me, are you still practising on quai Louis-Blériot? Unless you've kept your surgery on rue de Moscou . . . And that period at Fresnes prison a long time ago, I hope the repercussions weren't too onerous . . ." I almost burst out laughing, all alone there, in my corner. We don't grow any older. With the passing years, many people and things end up seeming so comical and ridiculous to you that you look upon them with the eyes of a child.

I spent a long time waiting at Le Condé that first time. She didn't come. One had to be patient. It would be for another day. I observed the customers. Most of them were no more than twenty-five years old and a nineteenth-century novelist, refer-ring to them, would have alluded to "bohemian student life". But very few of them, in my opinion, were enrolled at the Sorbonne or at the École des Mines. I have to admit that ob-serving them at close quarters made me feel anxious about their futures.

Two men came in, one very shortly after the other. Adamov and that dark-haired man with the smooth walk who had signed a few books under the name of Maurice Raphaël. I knew Adamov by sight. There was a time when he was at the Old Navy almost every day and you didn't forget the look on his face. I believe I did him a favour by getting his papers put in order, in the days when I still had a few connections at Special Branch. As for Maurice Raphaël, he was also a regular at the local bars. It was said that he had had some difficulties after the war, under another name. At that time, I was working for Blémant. The two of them came and propped up the bar. Maurice Raphaël remained standing, very upright, and Adamov had hoisted himself onto a stool, wincing painfully. He had not noticed my presence. In any case, would my face still mean anything to him? Three young people, one of them a blonde girl wearing a shabby raincoat and with a fringe, joined them at the bar. Maurice Raphaël offered round a pack of cigarettes and gazed at them with an amused smile. Adamov, for his part, displayed less familiarity. From his intense expression, you might have thought that he was vaguely frightened by them.

I had two passport photos of this Jacqueline Delanque in my pocket . . . In the days when I worked for Blémant, he was always surprised by my ability to identify people, no matter who. I only had to look at a face once for it to remain etched in my memory, and Blémant used to tease me about this gift for immediately recognising someone from afar, whether it was from an angle or even from behind. So I did not feel anxious in the least. As soon as she walked into Le Condé, I would know it was her.

Dr Vala turned in the direction of the bar, and our eyes met. He gave a friendly wave. I had a sudden desire to walk over to his table and tell him that I had a private question to ask him. I would have taken him aside and I would have shown him the passport photos: "Do you know this person?" It really would have been useful for me to hear a little more about this girl from one of the customers of Le Condé.

As soon as I discovered the address of her hotel, I made my way there. I had chosen the slack period of the afternoon. There would be more of a chance of her not being there. I hoped so, at least. I could then ask a few questions about her at reception. It was a sunny autumn day and I had decided to walk there. I had left the embankment and I was slowly making my way inland. In rue du Cherche-Midi, I had the sun in my eyes. I walked into Le Chien qui fume and I ordered a brandy. I was worried. From behind the windowpane, I gazed out on avenue du Maine. I needed to take the left-hand pavement, and I would arrive at my destination. No reason to be worried. As I walked along the avenue, I would recover my calm. I was almost certain she would be out and in any case I was not going into the hotel, this time, to ask questions. I would lurk around, just as though I was tracking someone. I had all the time I needed. I was paid to do this.

When I reached rue Cels, I decided to find out the truth. A quiet, dull street, which reminded me not so much of a village or a suburb, but of those mysterious zones known as "hinterlands". I walked straight up to the reception desk of the hotel. Nobody. I waited for ten minutes or so hoping that she would not make an appearance. A door opened and a dark-haired woman with short hair, dressed entirely in black, came to the reception desk. In a friendly voice, I said:

"It's to do with Jacqueline Delanque."

I thought she was registered here under her maiden name.

She smiled at me and took an envelope from one of the pigeonholes behind her.

"Are you Monsieur Roland?"

Who was this guy? I nodded vaguely, on the off chance. She handed me the envelope on which was written in blue ink: "For Roland". The envelope was not sealed. On a large sheet of paper, I read:

Roland, come and meet me after 5 o'clock at Le Condé. Otherwise, ring me on Auteuil 15-28 and leave a message.

It was signed Louki. The diminutive of Jacqueline?

I refolded the sheet of paper and slipped it into the envelope which I handed back to the dark-haired woman.

"Forgive me . . . There's been some confusion . . . This isn't for me."

Without a second thought, she returned the letter to the pigeonhole mechanically.

"Has Jacqueline Delanque lived here for long?"

She paused for a moment and she replied in an obliging tone of voice:

"For about a month."

"Alone?"

"Yes."

I could sense she was not bothered and was ready to reply to all my questions. She gazed at me with an expression of extreme weariness.

"Thank you," I said to her.

"Not at all."

I preferred not to linger. This Roland might turn up at any moment. I returned to avenue du Maine and followed it in the opposite direction to the one I had taken earlier. At Le Chien qui fume I ordered a brandy again. I looked up the address of Le Condé in the directory. It was in the Odéon district. Four o'clock in the afternoon, so I had a bit of time to spare. Then I rang Auteuil 15-28. A curt message reminded me of the voice of the talking clock: "This is La Fontaine garage . . . What may I do for you?" I asked for Jacqueline Delanque. "She's gone out for a moment . . . Is there a message?" I was tempted to put down the receiver, but I forced myself to reply: "No, no message. Thank you."

Above all, ascertain as precisely as possible the routes that people take, in order to understand them better. I repeated to myself in a low voice: "Hotel rue Cels. La Fontaine garage. Café Condé. Louki." And then, that part of Neuilly between the Bois de Boulogne and the Seine where that guy had arranged to meet me to talk about his wife, the woman known as Jacqueline Choureau, *née* Delanque.

I have forgotten who had advised him to get in touch with me. It doesn't matter. He had probably found my address in the directory. I had taken the métro well before the time we were due to meet. The line was direct. I had got off at Sablons and I had walked around the vicinity for almost half an hour. I was accustomed to reconnoitring places before plunging immediately into the heart of the matter. In the past, Blémant used to criticise me for this and reckoned I was wasting my time. Dive in, he would say to me, rather than skirt around the edge of the pool. Personally, I thought the opposite. No over-hasty movements, instead passivity and slowness, which allow you to enter gently into the spirit of places.

A smell of autumn and the countryside hovered in the air. I was walking along the avenue that skirts the Jardin d'Acclimatation, but on the left-hand side, the side with the woods and the riding track, and I should have liked it to have been a straightforward walk.

This Jean-Pierre Choureau had phoned me in a monotone voice to arrange a meeting. All he had led me to understand was that it was to do with his wife. As I drew closer to his home, I could see him walking, like me, along the riding track and past the Jardin d'Acclimatation riding school. How old was he? The timbre of his voice had struck me as youthful, but voices are always deceptive.

What tragedy or what marital hell would he drag me into? I felt utterly dispirited and I was no longer very sure whether I wanted to go to this meeting. I disappeared into the Bois in the direction of the Saint-James pond and the small lake that skaters use during the winter. I was the only person walking and I had the sense of being far away from Paris, somewhere in Sologne. Yet again, I managed to overcome despondency. A vague professional curiosity made me interrupt my walk through the woods and return to the outskirts of Neuilly. Sologne. Neuilly. I imagined long, rainy afternoons for these Choureaus in Neuilly. And down there, in Sologne, at twilight, you could hear the hunting horns. Did his wife ride sidesaddle? I burst out laughing as I recalled Blémant's remark: "You, Caisley, you set off too quickly. You should have written novels."

He lived at the very end, at the porte de Madrid, a modern building with a large glass entrance. He had told me to go to the back of the hall, to the left. I would see his name on the door. "It's a flat on the ground floor." I had been surprised by the sadness with which he pronounced "ground floor". After which, a long silence, as if he regretted this admission.

"And the exact address?" I had asked him.

"Eleven avenue de Bretteville. Have you got that? Eleven . . . At four o'clock – would that suit you?"

His voice had grown stronger and had almost taken on a sociable tone.

A small gilt plate on the door: Jean-Pierre Choureau, beneath which I noticed a spyhole. I rang. I waited. There, in this deserted, silent hallway, I reckoned that I had come too late. He had committed suicide. I was ashamed of such a thought and, once again, the longing to give it all up, to leave this hallway, and to continue my walk in the fresh air, in Sologne . . . I rang the bell again, three quick rings this time. The door opened immediately, as though he had been standing behind it, observing me through the spyhole.

A dark-haired man of about forty, hair cut short, and much taller than average. He was wearing a navy-blue suit and a pale blue shirt with an open collar. He led me towards what could be called the drawing room without saying a word. He pointed me to a sofa, behind a low table, and we sat there side by side. He had difficulty in speaking. To put him at his ease, I said to him in as gentle a voice as possible: "So, it's to do with your wife?"

He tried to adopt a casual tone. He shot me a weary smile. Yes, his wife had disappeared two months ago following a trivial quarrel. Was I the first person to whom he had spoken since this disappearance? The metal shutter in one of the bay windows was lowered, and I wondered whether this man had kept himself shut up in his apartment for two months. But apart from the shutter, there was no trace of disarray or slovenliness in this drawing room. He himself, after a moment's hesitancy, regained a degree of self-assurance.

"I hope that this business can be sorted out fairly quickly," he said to me eventually.

I observed him from closer quarters. Very clear eyes beneath black eyebrows, high cheekbones, a regular profile. And in his bearing and movement a sportsman's vitality that was accentuated by his short hair. One could easily have imagined him as a lone sailor aboard a yacht, stripped to the waist. And in spite of such apparent assurance and charm, his wife had left him.

I wanted to know whether in all this time he had made attempts to find her. No. She had telephoned him three or four times confirming that she would not be coming back anymore. She advised him in no uncertain terms not to try to get in touch with her and gave him no explanation. Her voice had changed. It was no longer the same person. A very calm, very self-assured voice that greatly perturbed him. There was a gap of about fifteen years between him and his wife. She was twenty-two. He, thirty-six. While he was giving me these details, I could sense a reticence about him, and even a coldness, which was probably the consequence of what they call a good education. Now, I had to put more and more specific questions to him and I no longer knew whether this was worthwhile. What did he actually want? For his wife to return? Or, quite simply, was he trying to understand why she had left him? Perhaps that was enough for him? Apart from the sofa and the low table, there was no furniture in the drawing room. The bay windows overlooked the avenue, where only the occasional car passed, so that it did not matter that the apartment was on the ground floor. Dusk was falling. He switched on the three-legged lamp with a red shade that stood beside the sofa, to my right. The light made me blink, a white light that made the silence even deeper. I think he was waiting for my questions. He had crossed his legs. To save time, I took out my spiral-bound notebook and my ballpoint pen from the inside pocket of my coat and I made a few notes. "He, 36 years of age. She, 22. Neuilly. Ground-floor apartment. No furniture. Bay windows overlooking avenue de Bretteville. No traffic. A few magazines on the low table." He waited without saying anything as though I were a doctor writing out a prescription.

"Your wife's maiden name?"

"Delanque. Jacqueline Delanque."

I asked him for the date and place of birth of this Jacqueline Delanque. The date, too, of their marriage. Did she have a driving licence? A regular job? No. Did she have any family? In Paris? In the country? A chequebook? As he replied to me in his sad voice, I noted down these details that are often the only evidence of a living person's transit on earth. Always provided that the spiral-bound notebook in which someone has recorded them in tiny barely legible handwriting, like mine, is found one day.

Now, I had to proceed to more delicate questions, the kind that oblige you to intrude on a person's privacy without asking their permission. By what right?

"Do you have friends?"

Yes, a few people whom he saw fairly regularly. He had known them at a business school. Some of them had actually been classmates, at the Jean-Baptiste-Say lycée.

He had even tried to start up a business with three of them before he became a senior partner at the property company Zannetacci.

"Do you still work there?"

"Yes. At 20 rue de la Paix."

By what means of transport did he travel to the office? Every detail, however seemingly insignificant, is revealing. By car. From time to time he went on trips for Zannetacci. Lyon. Bordeaux. The Côte d'Azur. Geneva. And was Jacqueline Choureau, *née* Delanque, left on her own at Neuilly? When these trips occurred, he had occasionally taken her to the Côte d'Azur. And when she was on her own, how did she occupy her leisure time? Was there really nobody who might conceivably be prepared to give him any information about the disappearance of Jacqueline, wife of Choureau, *née* Delanque, and provide him with the slightest clue? "I don't know, some secret she might have revealed one day when she was feeling downcast . . ." No. She would never have confided in anyone. She often criticised him for his own friends' lack of imagination. It also has to be said that she was fifteen years younger than all of them.

I was now coming to a question that bothered me initially, but which I was obliged to ask him:

"Do you think that she had a lover?"

The tone of my voice struck me as a little brusque and rather foolish. But that was how it was. He frowned.

"No."

He hesitated and looked me straight in the eyes as though he was looking for my support or was searching for words. One evening, one of the former friends from business school had come to dinner here with a certain Guy de Vere, a man who was older than them. This Guy de Vere was very conversant with the occult and had suggested bringing them a few books on the subject. His wife had taken part in several gatherings and even in sorts of conferences that this Guy de Vere held regularly. He had never been able to accompany her because of a surfeit of work at the Zannetacci office. His wife expressed interest in these gatherings and conferences and often spoke to him about them, without his understanding very well what they were about. Among the books that Guy de Vere had recommended to her, she had lent him the one that seemed to him to be the easiest to read. It was called *Lost Horizon*. Was he in contact with Guy de Vere after his wife's disappearance? Yes, he had telephoned him several times, but he had heard nothing. "Are you quite sure about that?" He shrugged and stared at me wearily. This Guy de Vere had been very evasive and he had realised that he was not going to obtain any information from him. The precise name and address of this man? He didn't know his address. It was not in the directory.

I tried to think of other questions to put to him. Silence between us, but this did not appear to bother him. Sitting side by side on this sofa, we could have been in a dentist's or doctor's waiting room. Bare white walls. A picture of a woman hanging above the sofa. I almost picked up one of the magazines on the low table. A feeling of emptiness came over me. I should say that at that moment I felt the absence of Jacqueline Choureau *née* Delanque to such a degree that it seemed to me conclusive. But I couldn't be pessimistic right at the beginning. And anyway, wouldn't this drawing room impart the same sense of emptiness when this woman was present? Did they have dinner there? If so, it was probably on a card table that could be folded and put away afterwards. I wanted to know whether she had left on a sudden impulse, leaving a few belongings behind. No. She had taken her clothes and the various books that Guy de Vere had lent her, and packed them all in a dark-red leather suitcase. Not the least trace of her remained here. Even the photographs in which she featured – some rare holiday photographs – had disappeared. In the evening, alone in this apartment, he wondered whether he had ever been married to this Jacqueline Delanque. The one proof that all of it had not been a dream was the family record book that had been given to them after their wedding. Family record book. He repeated these words, as though he no longer understood their meaning.

There was no point in my visiting the other rooms in the apartment. Empty bedrooms. Empty cupboards. And the silence, barely broken by a passing car on avenue de Bretteville. The evenings must be long.

"Did she leave with the key?"

He shook his head. Not even the hope of one night hearing the sound of the key in the lock that would herald her return home. And then it occurred to him that she would never ever telephone him again.

"How did you come to know her?"

She had been taken on at Zannetacci's to replace an employee who had left unexpectedly. A temp's job. He had dictated a few letters to customers to her and that was how they had got to know each other. They had met outside office hours. She had told him that she was a student at the École des Langues Orientales where she took courses twice a week, but he had not been able to discover exactly what language it was. Asiatic languages, she would say. And, after two months, they were married one Sunday morning at Neuilly town hall, with two colleagues from the Zannetacci office as witnesses. No-one else took part in what for him was merely a simple formality. They had gone to have lunch with the witnesses very close to his home, on the edge of the Bois de Boulogne, in a restaurant used by the customers of the nearby riding schools.

He gave me an awkward look. It was clear that he would have liked to give me further explanations about this marriage. I smiled at him. I didn't need explanations. He made an effort and, as though he were taking the plunge:

"We try to establish ties, you understand . . ."

Of course I understood. In this life that sometimes seems like a vast wasteland without any signpost, in the midst of all the escape routes and the lost horizons, we long to find reference points and establish a sort of land register so that we no longer have the sense of navigating aimlessly. So, we construct ties, we try to make chance encounters more stable. I said nothing, my gaze concentrated on the pile of magazines. In the middle of the low table was a large yellow ashtray bearing the inscription Cinzano. And a paperback, the title of which was *Adieu Focolara*. Zannetacci, Jean-Pierre Choureau. Cinzano. Jacqueline Delanque. Neuilly town hall. Focolara. And one was supposed to find a meaning in all this.

"And then she was someone who was attractive . . . For me it was love at first sight . . ."

No sooner had he confided this in a low voice than he seemed to regret it. In the days that had preceded her disappearance, had he sensed anything particular about her? Well, yes, she was reproaching him more and more often about their day-to-day life. This was not real life, she used to say. And when he asked her what exactly "real life" consisted of, she shrugged without answering, as though she knew he would not have a clue about her explanations. And then she rediscovered her smile and her kindness and she almost apologised for her bad mood. She adopted a resigned look and she told him that basically none of this mattered very much. One day, perhaps, he would discover what "real life" was.

"Do you really not have a single photograph of her?"

One afternoon, they were walking beside the Seine. He was planning to take the métro at Châtelet to go back to his office. On boulevard du Palais, they had passed the little Photomaton booth. She needed photographs for a new passport. He had waited for her on the pavement. When she came out, she had entrusted the photographs to him, saying she was frightened of losing them. When he was back in his office, he had put these photographs in an envelope and had forgotten to take them home to Neuilly. After his wife had disappeared, he had noticed that the envelope was still there, on his desk, among other office documents.

"Will you wait for me a moment?"

He left me alone on the sofa. It was dark. I looked at my watch and I was astonished that the hands only pointed to a quarter to six. I had the impression of having been there much longer.

Two photographs in a grey envelope on which was printed, on the left-hand side: "Immobilière Zannetacci (France), 20 rue de la Paix, Paris Ier." One photograph full-face, the other in profile, as the police headquarters used to require for foreigners. The name Delanque, and the first name Jacqueline, were, however, very French. Two photographs which I held between thumb and forefinger and which I gazed at in silence. Brown hair, bright eyes, and one of those profiles so pure they even make anthropometric photographs look attractive. And both of these had all the dullness and indifference of anthropometric photographs.

"Will you lend them to me for a while?" I asked him.

"Of course."

I shoved the envelope into my coat pocket.

There comes a moment when one should not listen to anyone any longer. What did he, Jean-Pierre Choureau, know exactly about Jacqueline Delanque? Not much. They had lived together in this ground-floor apartment in Neuilly for barely a year. They used to sit side by side on this sofa, they had dinner sitting opposite one another and sometimes with former friends from the business school and the Jean-Baptiste-Say lycée. Was that enough to deduce everything that is going on inside somebody's head? Did she see members of her family? I had made a final attempt to ask him this question.

"No. She had no family left."

I got to my feet. He gave me an anxious look, but remained sitting on the sofa.

"It's time for me to leave," I told him. "It's late."

I smiled at him, but he seemed genuinely surprised that I should want to leave him.

"I'll phone you as soon as possible," I said to him. "I hope to be able to give you some news shortly."

He then got to his feet, moving at that sleepwalker's pace with which he had guided me into the drawing room earlier. One last question came to mind:

"Did she leave with any money?"

"No."

"And when she phoned you, after she had run away, did she not give you any information about how she was living?"

"No."

He was walking stiffly towards the front door. Was he still capable of replying to my questions? I opened the door. He was standing stock-still behind me. I don't know what dizzy spell came over me, what flash of bitterness, but I said to him abruptly:

"You were probably expecting to grow old with her?"

Was it to arouse him from his torpor and his despondency? His eyes opened wide and he looked at me fearfully. I was standing in the doorway. I moved towards him and put my hand on his shoulder:

"Don't hesitate to ring me. At whatever time."

His face grew more relaxed. He managed to smile. Before closing the door, he gave me a wave. I stood there in the hallway for a long while, and the time-switch ran out. I imagined him sitting by himself on the sofa, in the position he had occupied earlier. Instinctively, he picked up one of the magazines piled up on the low table.

*

Outside, it was dark. I could not rid my mind of that man in his ground-floor apartment, under the harsh lighting. Would he have anything to eat before going to bed? I wondered whether there was a kitchen there. I should have invited him to dinner. Perhaps, without my asking him any questions, he might have uttered a word or an admission that could have put me on the trail of Jacqueline Delanque sooner. Blémant was always telling me that there comes a moment for each individual, even the most stubborn, when he "spills the beans": those were the words he always used. It was up to us to wait extremely patiently for that moment, while trying, of course, to bring it about, though in an almost imperceptible way, Blémant used to say, "with small, delicate pinpricks". The guy should be under the impression that he is face to face with a confidant. It was difficult. It was our job. I had reached Porte Maillot and I wanted to go on walking for a while longer in the warmth of the evening. Unfortunately, my new shoes were hurting me badly on the instep. So I walked into the first café on the avenue and chose one of the tables near the bay window. I unlaced my shoes and removed the one on the left foot, which was the more painful. When the waiter came, I did not resist the brief moment of sweetness and forgetfulness that a green Izarra would provide me with.

I took the envelope from my pocket and studied the two passport photographs at length. Where was she now? In a café, like me, sitting at a table on her own? It was probably the remark he had uttered earlier that had given me this notion: "We try to establish ties . . ." Meetings in a street, at a métro station during rush hour. We ought to handcuff ourselves to one another at moments like that. What tie could resist that stream that sweeps you up and causes you to drift off? An anonymous office where you dictate a letter to a temporary typist, a ground-floor apartment in Neuilly whose bare white walls remind you of what is known as "a show flat" and where you leave no trace of your having been there . . . Two passport photographs, one full-face, the other in profile . . . And that's all you have to establish ties? There was someone who could help me in my search: Bernolle. I had not seen him since the Blémant period, apart from one afternoon three years ago. I was heading for the métro and was walking across the forecourt of Notre-Dame. A tramp-like figure came out of the Hôtel-Dieu and our paths crossed. He was wearing a raincoat with torn sleeves, trousers that stopped above his ankles, and his bare feet were clad in old sandals. He was unshaven and his black hair was far too long. I recognised him nonetheless. Bernolle. I followed him with the intention of speaking to him. But he was walking too quickly. He vanished through the large doorway of the police headquarters. I paused for a moment. It was too late to catch up with him. So, I decided to wait for him, there, on the pavement. After all, we had been young together.

He emerged from the same door in a navy-blue overcoat, flannel trousers and black lace-up shoes. It was no longer the same man. He seemed embarrassed when I accosted him. He was freshly shaven. We walked along the embankment without saying anything. Once we were seated at a table at Le Soleil d'Or a little further on, he confided in me. He was still employed for intelligence tasks, oh, nothing very much, informer and mole work which involved working with tramps in order to see and hear what was going on around him: staking out buildings, in flea markets, in Pigalle, around stations and even in the Latin Quarter. He smiled sadly. He lived in a studio flat in the 16th arrondissement. He gave me his telephone number. Not for one moment did we speak about the past. He had put his overnight bag on the bench beside him. He would have been very surprised if I had told him what it contained: an old raincoat, trousers that were too short, a pair of sandals.

*

On the same evening that I returned from that meeting in Neuilly, I telephoned him. Ever since we had got together again, I had occasionally turned to him for information that I needed. I asked him to find out a few details for me concerning the woman known as Jacqueline Delanque, wife of Choureau. I did not have much to tell him about this person other than the date of her birth and that of her marriage to a certain Choureau, Jean-Pierre, 11 avenue de Bretteville in Neuilly, a senior partner at Zannetacci's. He took note. "Is that all?" He sounded disappointed. "And nothing in the police files about these people, I suppose?" he said in a contemptuous voice. Police files. I tried to imagine the Choureaus' bedroom at Neuilly, a room I should have glanced at as a matter of professional principle. A room that was empty forever, a bed of which all that remained was the mattress base.

Over the following weeks, Choureau telephoned me several times. He always spoke in a monotone and it was always seven o'clock in the evening. Perhaps at that time, alone in his ground-floor apartment, he needed to speak to someone. I told him to be patient. I had the impression that he no longer had any self-belief and that he would gradually come to accept his wife's disappearance. I received a letter from Bernolle:

My dear Caisley,

Nothing in the files. Either about Choureau or about Delanque.

But there are some lucky coincidences: a tiresome study of statistics of the daybooks of police stations in the 9th and 18th arrondissements that I was asked to carry out has enabled me to find out some bits of information for you.

On two occasions, I came across "Delanque, Jacqueline, aged 15". The first time, in the daybook of the police station of the Saint-Georges district from seven years ago, and a second time, a few months later, in that of the Grandes-Carrières district. Reason: Juvenile vagrancy.

I asked Leoni if there might be anything regarding hotels. Two years ago, Delanque Jacqueline lived in the Hôtel San Remo, 8 rue d'Armaillé (17th) and the Hôtel Métropole, 13 rue de l'Étoile (17th). In the Saint-Georges and Grandes-Carrières daybooks it is stated that she resided with her mother, 10 avenue Rachel (18th arrondissement).

She currently lives at the Hôtel Savoie, 8 rue Cels, in the 14th arrondissement. Her mother died four years ago. On her birth certificate from the mairie of Fontaines-en-Sologne (Loir-et-Cher), a copy of which I'm sending you, it is mentioned that she was born of an unknown father. Her mother was employed as an usherette at the Moulin-Rouge and had a friend, a certain Guy Lavigne, who worked at the La Fontaine garage, 98 rue La Fontaine (16th) and helped her financially. Jacqueline Delanque does not appear to have a regular job.

Well, that is all I've obtained for you, my dear Caisley. I hope to see you soon, but on condition that it's not when I'm wearing my work clothes. Blémant would have laughed a great deal over that tramp's disguise. You, rather less, I imagine. And I, not at all.

Good luck,

Bernolle

All that remained was for me to telephone Jean-Pierre Choureau to tell him that the mystery had been cleared up. I am trying to remember at what precise moment I decided not to do anything about it. I had dialled the first digits of his number when I stopped. I was oppressed by the prospect of returning to that ground-floor apartment in Neuilly in the late afternoon like last time, and waiting with him, beneath the lamp with the red shade, for dusk to fall. I unfolded the old Taride map of Paris that I always keep on my desk, within easy reach. Through referring to it constantly, I have many a time torn it around the edges and, on each occasion, I would stick Sellotape over the tear, just as one dresses a wound. Le Condé. Neuilly. The Étoile district. Avenue Rachel. For the first time in my professional life, I experienced the need to go against the flow in my investigation. Yes, I was making the journey that Jacqueline Delanque had made, in the opposite direction. As for Jean-Pierre Choureau, he no longer mattered. His had only been a walk-on part and I watched him disappearing for good, a black towel in his hand, in the direction of the Zannatacci office. The only interesting person, in fact, was Jacqueline Delanque. There had been many Jacquelines in my life . . . She would be the last. I took the métro, the North–South line, as it was known, the one that connected avenue Rachel to Le Condé. As the stations passed by, I went back in time. I got off at Pigalle. And there I walked along the central divide of the boulevard with a light step. A sunny afternoon in autumn when you could have made plans for the future and when you could start life all over again. After all, it was in this area that Jacqueline Delanque's life had begun , , , I felt as though I had a rendezvous with her. At the top of place Blanche, my heart was beating slightly faster and I felt unsettled and even nervous. I had not experienced this for a long time. I continued to walk along at an ever brisker pace. In this familiar neighbourhood, I could have walked with my eyes shut: the Moulin-Rouge, Le Sanglier Bleu . . . Who knows? I had passed this Jacqueline Delanque a long time ago, on the right-hand pavement as she went to meet her mother at the Moulin-Rouge, or on the left-hand pavement at the time when the Jules-Ferry lycée came out. There, I had arrived. I had forgotten the cinema at the corner of the avenue. It was called Le Mexico and it was no coincidence that it had such a name. It gave you a longing for journeys, for running away or escaping . . . I had also forgotten the silence and the calm of avenue Rachel that leads to the cemetery, but you don't think of the cemetery there, you tell yourself that right at the very end you will emerge in the countryside, and even with a bit of luck on a seaside promenade.

I stopped outside number 10 and, after a moment's hesitation, I entered the building. I intended to knock at the concierge's glass door, but I held back. What was the point? In black letters, on a small card stuck to one of the door panels, were the names of the tenants and the floors on which each of them lived. I took my notebook and ballpoint pen from the inside pocket of my coat and I jotted down the names:

Deyrlord (Christiane)
Dix (Gisèle)
Dupuy (Marthe)
Esnault (Yvette)
Gravier (Alice)
Manoury (Albine)
Mariska
Van Bosterhaudt (Huguette)
Zazani (Odette)

The name Delanque (Geneviève) was crossed out and replaced by Van Bosterhaudt (Huguette). The mother and daughter had lived on the fifth floor. But as I closed the notebook I knew that all these details would be of no use to me.

Outside, on the ground floor of the building, a man was standing in the doorway of a draper's shop at the sign of La

Licorne. As I looked up to the fifth floor, I heard him say to me in a reedy voice:

"Are you looking for something, sir?"

I ought to have asked him a question about Geneviève and Jacqueline Delanque, but I knew what his answer would have been, nothing but very superficial, tiny "surface" details, as Blémant used to say, that never went any deeper. One only had to hear his reedy voice and observe his nosy-parker face and the severity of his gaze: no, there was nothing to hope for from him, apart from the "intelligence" that a mere informer could provide. Or else, he would tell me that he knew neither Geneviève nor Jacqueline Delanque. Confronted by this fellow with his weasel face, a cold anger swept over me. Perhaps he had come to represent for me all those many so-called witnesses whom I had questioned during my investigations and who, out of stupidity, spite or indifference, had never understood a thing about what they had seen. I walked over with a heavy tread and stood right in front of him. I was twenty centimetres taller than him and twice his weight.

"Is there a law against looking at the fronts of buildings?"

He glared at me with a hard and fearful stare. I wish I could have made him even more frightened.

And then, to calm myself down, I went and sat on a bench on the central divide, on a level with the beginning of the avenue, opposite Le Mexico cinema. I took off my left shoe.

Sunshine. I was lost in my thoughts. Jacqueline Delanque could rely on my discretion, Choureau would never know anything about the Hôtel Savoie, Le Condé, the La Fontaine garage and the person called Roland, who was no doubt the dark-haired man with a suede jacket mentioned in the note-book. "Louki. Monday 12 February 11.00 p.m. Louki 28 April 2.00 p.m. Louki with the dark-haired guy in suede jacket." As I went through the pages of this notebook, I had underlined her name in blue pencil each time, and copied out, on loose-leaf pages, all the notes that concerned her. With the dates. And the times. But she had no reason to be anxious. I would not go back to Le Condé anymore. Truly, I had been lucky on the two or three times that I waited for her at one of the tables in this café that she did not turn up that day. I would have been embarrassed to have spied on her without her being aware of it; yes, I would have been ashamed of my role. By what right do we break into people's lives and what an impertinence to probe their hearts and minds – and to ask them for explanations – on what grounds? I had taken off my sock and was massaging my instep. The pain subsided. Dusk had fallen. In the past, it was the time, I imagine, that Geneviève Delanque set off to her job at the Moulin-Rouge. Her daughter remained on her own, on the fifth floor. At the age of about thirteen or fourteen, one evening, after her mother's departure, she had left the building, taking great care not to attract the attention of the concierge. Once outside, she had gone no further than the corner of the avenue. To begin with, she had been happy just to attend the ten o'clock showing at Le Mexico cinema. Then it was back to the building, going up the stairs, without turning on the time-switch, and the door that had to be closed as quietly as possible. One night, after leaving the cinema, she had walked a little further, as far as place Blanche. And every night, a little bit further. Juvenile vagrancy, as it was described in the daybooks of the Saint-Georges and Grandes-Carrières districts, and those two words reminded me of a meadow in the moonlight, beyond the Caulaincourt bridge right down there behind the cemetery, a meadow where you could breathe fresh air at last. Her mother had come to collect her from the police station. From now on, things gathered momentum and no-one could restrain her anymore. Nocturnal wanderings towards the west, if I am to judge by the few clues that Bernolle had assembled. Initially, the Étoile neighbourhood, and still further west, Neuilly and the Bois de Boulogne. But then why had she married Choureau? And another escape, but this time in the direction of the Left Bank, as if crossing over the river might protect her from an imminent danger. And yet had this marriage not also been a protection for her? If she had had the patience to remain in Neuilly, one would have eventually forgotten that behind a Mme Jean-Pierre Choureau there was hiding a Jacqueline Delanque whose name featured in police-station daybooks on two occasions.

Clearly, I was still a slave to my old professional instincts, those that led me to tell my colleagues that, even in my sleep, I was pursuing my enquiries. Blémant compared me to that post-war gangster who was known as "the man who smoked while he slept". On his bedside table he kept an ashtray on which a lit cigarette was placed. He slept in fits and starts and, each time he briefly awoke, he would reach out to the ashtray and take a puff. And once he had done this, moving like a sleepwalker, he would light another. But in the morning, he remembered none of this and was convinced he had slept deeply. Sitting on this bench, now that it was dark, I too had the sense of being in a dream in which I continued following the tracks of Jacqueline Delanque.

Or rather, I felt her presence on this boulevard where the lights gleamed like signals, without my being able to decipher them very clearly and without really knowing which years they referred to. And these lights seemed even brighter to me, because of the darkness of the central divide. Simultaneously bright and distant.

I had pulled on my sock, thrust my foot into my left shoe again and left this bench where I would gladly have spent the entire night. And I was walking along the central divide like her, at the age of fifteen, before she was caught. Where and at what moment had she drawn attention to herself?

Jean-Pierre Choureau would eventually grow weary. I would still respond to him occasionally on the telephone and give him some vague pieces of information – all untruthful, of course. Paris is big and it is easy to lose someone there. When I have the sense of having lured him onto false tracks, I shall no longer answer his calls. Jacqueline could depend on me. I would allow her time to put herself permanently out of reach.

At this moment, she too was walking somewhere in this city. Or else she was sitting at a table, at Le Condé. But she had nothing to fear. I would no longer be at the meeting.

WHEN I WAS FIFTEEN, PEOPLE USED TO THINK I WAS NINE-
teen. And even twenty. My name was not Louki, but Jacqueline. I was even younger the first time I took advantage of my
mother's absence and went out. She would set off for work
at about nine o'clock in the evening and she did not return
before two in the morning. That first time, I had a lie ready in
case the con-cierge caught me unawares on the staircase. I
would have told her that I needed to buy medicine from the
chemist's on place Blanche.

I had not been back to the neighbourhood until the evening when Roland took me by taxi to the home of that friend of
Guy de Vere's. We used to have meetings there with all those
who normally came to the gatherings. We had just got to know
one another, Roland and I, and I hadn't dared say anything to

him when he asked the taxi to stop in place Blanche. He wanted us to walk. He may not have noticed how I clasped his arm. I was feeling dizzy. I had the impression that if I were to cross the square, I would keel over. I was frightened. He, who often talks to me about Eternal Recurrence, would have understood. Yes, everything was beginning again for me, as though the meeting with these people was merely a pretext and they had asked Roland to lead me gently back to the fold.

I was relieved that we did not go past the Moulin-Rouge. And yet my mother had been dead for four years and I had nothing to fear any longer. Each time that I escaped from the apartment at night, when she was out, I would walk on the other pavement of the boulevard, the 9th arrondissement side. No light on that pavement. The gloomy Jules-Ferry lycée building, then the frontages of buildings with darkened windows, a restaurant, though it always seemed to be in semi-darkness. And, each time, I could not prevent myself sneaking a glance at the other side of the central divide, at the Moulin-Rouge. When I reached the Café des Palmiers and came out onto place Blanche, I felt rather worried. There were lights, once more. One night when I was walking past the chemist's, I saw my mother with other customers, through the window. I imagined that she must have finished her work earlier than usual and that she would be returning to the apartment. If I ran, I would get there before her. I went and stood on the corner of rue de Bruxelles to see which way she would be going. But she had crossed the square and was walking back to the Moulin-Rouge.

I often felt frightened, and I would happily have gone to see my mother to calm myself down, but I would have disturbed her at work. Today, I feel sure that she would not have scolded me, because on the night that she came to collect me from the Grandes-Carrières police station, she did not blame me, threaten me or start moralising. We walked in silence. In the middle of the Caulaincourt bridge, I heard her murmur casually, "my poor girl", but I wasn't sure whether she was talking to me or to herself. She waited for me to get undressed and for me to get into bed before coming into my bedroom. She sat at the foot of the bed and she continued to say nothing. So did I. Eventually, she smiled. She said to me, "We're not great chatterboxes . . .", and she looked me in the eye. It was the first time she had kept her gaze on me for so long and the first time I had noticed how clear, how grey or pale blue her eyes were. Greyish-blue. She leant over and kissed me on the cheek, or rather I felt her lips doing so surreptitiously. And still that intent and absent-minded gaze fixed on me. She switched off the light and before shutting the door she said to me: "Try not to do it again." I think it was the only time there was an intimacy between us. It was so brief, so awkward and yet so strong that I regretted, in the months that followed, not having had a surge of feeling towards her that might have aroused this intimacy again. But neither of us were especially demonstrative people. Perhaps she had this apparently indifferent attitude towards me because she had no illusions about me. She probably told herself that there was not much to hope for since I was just like her.

But I never thought of this at the time. I lived in the present without asking myself questions. Everything changed on the evening Roland brought me back to this neighbourhood that I used to avoid. I had not set foot there since my mother's death. The taxi turned into rue de la Chaussée-d'Antin and, at the far end, I saw the dark mass of La Trinité church, like a gigantic eagle standing guard. I felt ill at ease. We were approaching the frontier. I told myself that there was hope. We might perhaps fork off to the right. But no. We were driving straight ahead, we were passing the square de la Trinité and were going up the hill. At the traffic lights, before reaching place de Clichy, I nearly opened the car door and ran away. But I couldn't do that to him.

It was later on, as we were walking along rue des Abbesses towards the apartment where we had our meeting, that I recovered my calm. Fortunately, Roland had not noticed anything. I regretted then that we could not have walked for longer in the neighbourhood, the two of us. I should have liked to have shown him around and let him see the place where I had lived barely six years earlier and which now seemed so long ago, in another life . . . After my mother died, only one tie connected me to this period, a certain Guy Lavigne, my mother's friend. I had understood that it was he who paid the rent for the apartment. I still see him, from time to time. He works in a garage, in Auteuil. But we scarcely ever talk about the past. He is as uncommunicative as my mother. When they took me to the police station, they asked me questions I was obliged to answer but, to begin with, I did so with such reluctance that they said to me, "You're not very talkative," just as they would have said to my mother and to Guy Lavigne had they ever been in their hands. I was not used to being asked questions. I was even astonished that they should be interested in me. The second time, at the Grandes-Carrières police station, I came across a copper who was nicer than the previous one and I liked his way of asking me questions. You were allowed to confide in him, for example, to talk about yourself, and someone sitting opposite you was interested in everything you said and did. I was so unused to this situation that I could not find the words to reply. Apart from specific questions. For example: Where were you at school? The nuns at Saint-Vincent de Paul in rue Caulaincourt and the primary school in rue Antoinette. I was ashamed to tell him that I had not been accepted at the Jules-Ferry lycée, but I took a deep breath and I confessed. He leant over towards me and said in a gentle voice, as though he wished to comfort me: "Tough luck on the Jules-Ferry lycée . . ." And that gave me such a surprise that at first I wanted to laugh. He smiled at me and looked me straight in the eyes, a look that was as clear as my mother's, but more affectionate, more thoughtful. He also asked me about my family situation. I felt safe with him and managed to communicate a few bits of information: my mother came from a village in the Sologne, the place where M. Foucret, the manager of the Moulin-Rouge, had a property. And it was because of this that at a very young age, when she came up to Paris, she had got a job in this organisation. I didn't know who my father was. I was born down in the Sologne, but we had never gone back there. That's why my mother often used to say to me: "We've no longer got a framework . . ." He listened to me and occasionally took some notes. As for me, I experienced a novel sensation: as I was giving him these pathetic details, a weight was lifted from me. None of this concerned me any longer, I was talking about someone else and I was reassured to see that he took notes. If everything was down in black and white, it meant that it was over, just like tombstones that have names and dates carved on them. And I was talking more and more quickly, and the words kept getting jumbled up: Moulin-Rouge, my mother, Guy Lavigne, Jules-Ferry lycée, the Sologne . . . I had never been able to speak to anyone. What a relief as all these words came tumbling out of my mouth . . . A part of my life was coming to an end, a life that had been imposed on me. From now on, I would be the one to decide my own fate. Everything would begin from this day on, and to get a really good head-start, I should have preferred him to cross out what he had just written down. I was prepared to give him further details and other names and to talk to him about an imaginary family, the sort of family I would have dreamt of having.

At about two o'clock in the morning, my mother came to fetch me. He told her that it wasn't very serious. He was still watching me with his thoughtful expression. Juvenile vagrancy, that was what was written in their register. Outside, the taxi was waiting. When he had asked me questions about my schooling, I had forgotten to tell him that for a few months I had attended a school a little further along on the same pavement as the police station. I would stay behind in the canteen and my mother came to collect me in the late afternoon. Sometimes, she was late arriving and I used to wait for her, sitting on a bench on the central divide. It was there that I noticed the street had different names on either side of the road. And that same night, she had also come to collect me, very close to the school, but this time from the police station. An odd sort of street that had two names and seemed to want to play a role in my life . . .

From time to time my mother glanced anxiously at the taxi meter. She told the driver to stop at the corner of rue Caulaincourt, and when she took coins from her purse, I realised that she only had just enough to pay for the journey. We walked the rest of the way. I walked more quickly than she did and she trailed behind me. Then I stopped so that she could catch up with me. On the bridge that overlooks the cemetery and from which you can see our building below, we stopped for a long time and I had the impression that she was recovering her breath. "You walk too quickly," she told me. Today, a thought occurs to me. Perhaps I was trying to lead her a bit beyond her own restricted life. Were she not dead, I believe I would have succeeded in broadening her horizons.

In the three or four years that followed, it was often the same routes and the same streets, and yet I went further and further afield. To begin with, I did not even walk as far as place Blanche. I barely went round the block . . . First, that tiny cinema, on the corner of the boulevard a few yards from the building, where the programme began at ten o'clock in the evening. The auditorium was empty, except on Saturdays. The films were set in faraway countries, such as Mexico and Arizona. I paid no attention to the plot, only the landscape interested me. On the way out, there was a strange fusion in my head between Arizona and boulevard de Clichy. The colours of the bright neon signs were the same as those in the film: orange, emerald green, midnight blue, sandy yellow, colours that were too violent and gave me the sense of still being in the film or in a dream. A dream or a nightmare, it depended. To begin with, a nightmare, because I was frightened and I didn't dare go much further. And it wasn't because of my mother. Had she discovered me all alone on the boulevard, at midnight, there would scarcely have been a word of criticism. In her calm voice, she would have told me to go back to the apartment, as though she were not at all astonished to see me outside at this late hour. I think that I walked on the other pavement, the shady side, because I felt that there was nothing more my mother could do for me.

The first time they carted me off was in the 9th arrondissement, at the beginning of rue de Douai, in that bakery that stays open all night. It was already one o'clock in the morning. I was standing at one of those tall tables and I was eating a croissant. After that time, you can always find strange people in this bakery, and they often come from the café opposite, Le Sans-Souci. Two plainclothes coppers came in to carry out an identity check. I didn't have any papers and they wanted to know my age. I preferred to tell them the truth. They made me get into the police van with a tall blond guy who was wearing a reverse sheepskin jacket. He appeared to know the policemen. Perhaps he was one. At one moment, he offered me a cigarette, but one of the plainclothes cops stopped him: "She's too young . . . it's bad for your health." And I believe they said "*tu*" when they spoke to him.

In the police station, they asked me my surname, my first name, my date of birth and my address, and they jotted these down on a register. I explained to them that my mother worked at the Moulin-Rouge. "Then, we're going to phone her", said one of the plainclothesmen. The man who was writing in the register gave him the number of the Moulin-Rouge. He dialled it, looking me straight in the eyes. I felt embarrassed. He said: "May I speak to Mme Geneviève Delanque?" He was still staring at me with a harsh expression and I lowered my gaze. And then, I heard: "No . . . Don't bother her . . ." He rang off. Now, he was smiling at me. He had wanted to frighten me. "It's okay on this occasion, but next time I'll be obliged to tell your mother." He stood up and we left the police station. The blond guy with the reverse sheepskin jacket was waiting on the pavement. They made me get into the car, in the back. "I'll take you home", the plainclothes cop told me. Now he was calling me "*tu*". The blond guy with the reverse sheepskin got out of the car at place Blanche, outside the chemist's. It was weird finding one-self alone on the back seat of a car with this guy driving. He stopped outside the entrance to the building. "Get some sleep. And don't do it again." He was addressing me formally again. I think I mumbled a "Thank you, monsieur". I walked over to the double door and, as I opened it, I glanced round. He had switched off the engine and he hadn't stopped watching me, as though he wanted to be sure that I was safely inside the building. I looked through my bedroom window. The car was still there. I waited, my forehead glued to the window, curious to know how long it would stay there. I heard the sound of the engine before it turned and disappeared around the corner of the street. I experienced that feeling of anxiety that often came over me at night and which was even stronger than fear – that feeling of being left on my own now without anyone to turn to. Neither my mother nor anyone else. I should have liked him to stay on guard all night outside the building, all night long and all the following nights, like a sentry, or rather a guardian angel who would watch over me.

But, on other evenings, the anxiety vanished and I waited impatiently for my mother to leave so that I could go out. I walked down the stairs with my heart thumping, as if I were going on a date. No longer any need to tell the concierge a fib, to find excuses or ask for permission. Who from? And why? I wasn't even sure that I would be coming back to the apartment. Outside, I did not take the pavement on the shady side of the road, but the one on the Moulin-Rouge side. The lights seemed even more glaring than those in the films about Mexico. A light-headedness came over me, so slight . . . I had experienced a similar feeling the evening I had drunk a glass of champagne in

Le Sans-Souci. I had my life before me. How had I been able to shrivel up and keep a low profile? And what had I been frightened of? I was going to meet people. All I had to do was go into any café.

I knew a girl, a little older than me, whose name was Jeannette Gaul. One night, when I was suffering from a bad headache, I had gone into the chemist's on place Blanche to buy some Veganin and a bottle of ether. When I came to pay, I realised that I hadn't any money. This blonde girl with short hair, who was wearing a raincoat and whose eyes had met mine – green eyes – walked over to the check-out and paid for me. I felt embarrassed, I didn't know how to thank her. I suggested taking her back to the apartment so I could reimburse her. I always had a little money in my bedside table. She said to me: "No . . . no . . . next time." She also lived in the neighbourhood, but lower down. She looked at me with her smiling green eyes. She suggested I have a drink with her, near where she lived, and we met in a café – or rather a bar – in rue de La Rochefoucauld. Not at all the same atmosphere as Le Condé. The walls were made of pale wood, as were the counter and the tables, and a sort of stained-glass window gave onto the street. Dark-red velvet benches. Subdued lighting. Behind the bar stood a blonde woman of about forty whom this Jeannette Gaul knew well since she called her Suzanne and addressed her as "*tu*". She served us two Pimm's with champagne.

"Your good health," Jeannette Gaul said to me. She was still smiling at me and I had the feeling that her green eyes were scrutinising me to discover what was going on inside my head. She asked me:

"Do you live locally?"

"Yes. A bit higher up."

There were numerous zones in the neighbourhood and I knew all their boundaries, even the invisible ones. Because I felt nervous and didn't really know what to say, I added: "Yes, I live higher up. Here, we're only on the first slopes." She frowned. "The first slopes?" These two words puzzled her, but she hadn't lost her smile. Was it the effect of the Pimm's and champagne? My shyness had melted. I explained to her what "the first slopes" meant, an expression that I had learnt as did all the children from the neighbourhood schools. "The first slopes" begin at square de la Trinité. You continue to climb until you get to the Château des Brouillards and the Saint-Vincent cemetery, before descending again towards the hinterland of Clignancourt, in the very north.

"You know a thing or two," she said to me. And her smile became ironic. She had called me "*tu*" straight away, but that struck me as natural. She ordered two more glasses from the woman called Suzanne. I wasn't used to alcohol and one glass was already too much for me. But I didn't dare refuse. To finish it more quickly, I swallowed the champagne down in one gulp. She was still observing me, in silence.

"Are you studying?"

I hesitated before replying. I had always dreamt of being a student, because of the word, which I thought was stylish. But this dream had become unrealisable for me the day they turned me down at the Jules-Ferry lycée. Was it the self-confidence that the champagne gave me? I leant over towards her and, perhaps to appear more convincing, I drew my face closer to hers:

"Yes, I'm a student."

On this first occasion, I didn't notice the customers around us. Nothing like Le Condé. If I wasn't frightened of coming across certain ghosts, I would happily return to this place one night so as to understand properly where I'm coming from. But one has to be careful. In any case, I might not find anybody there. Change of ownership. There was not much future in any of this.

"Student of what?"

She caught me unawares. The ingenuousness of her expression reassured me. She could certainly not think I was lying.

"In oriental languages."

She seemed impressed. She never asked me subsequently any details about my studies in oriental languages, neither the times of my courses, nor where the school was situated. She must have realised that I didn't attend any school. But in my opinion, for her – and for me too – it was a sort of title that I wore, the kind that one inherits without the need to do anything. To those who frequented the bar in rue de La Rochefoucauld, she introduced me as "the Student" and perhaps they still remember me there.

That night, she accompanied me home. I, in turn, had wanted to know what she did with her life. She told me that she had been a dancer, but that following an accident she had had to give up this career. A classical dancer? No, not exactly, and yet she had trained as a classical dancer. Today, I ask myself a question that would never have occurred to me at the time: Had she been any more a dancer than I had been a student? We were walking along rue Fontaine in the direction of place Blanche. She explained to me that "for the time being" she was "in partnership" with the woman called Suzanne, an old friend of hers and rather like her "big sister". Both of them looked after the place that she had taken me to that evening, which was also a restaurant.

She asked me whether I lived alone. Yes, alone with my mother. She wanted to know what job my mother did. I didn't say the words "Moulin-Rouge". I replied curtly: "Chartered accountant". After all, my mother could have been a chartered accountant. She had the gravity and the tact.

We said goodbye to one another by the main door. I didn't much enjoy coming back to this flat every night. I knew that sooner or later I would leave it for good. I relied a very great deal on the people I was going to meet, who would put an end to my loneliness. This girl was the first person I'd met and perhaps she would help me to break free.

"Shall we see each other tomorrow?" She seemed astonished by my question. I had asked it too suddenly, without managing to conceal my anxiety.

"Of course. Whenever you like . . ."

She smiled at me affectionately and ironically, just as she had done previously, the time I was explaining to her what "the first slopes" meant.

I have lapses of memory. Or rather certain details come back to me in a jumble. For five years, I didn't want to think about all that again. And it was enough for the taxi to go along the street for me to recognise the neon signs – Aux Noctambules, Aux Pierrots . . . I no longer remember what the place in rue de La Rochefoucauld was called. Le Rouge Cloître? Chez Dante? Le Canter? Yes, Le Canter. No customer of Le Condé would have spent time in Le Canter. There are impassable frontiers in life. And yet I had been very surprised on my first visits to Le Condé to recognise a customer I had seen at Le Canter, the guy known as Maurice Raphaël, whom they nickname the Jaguar . . . I really would not have guessed that this man was a writer . . . There was nothing to distinguish him from those who were playing cards and other games in the small room at the back, behind the wrought-iron grille . . . I recognised him. I didn't feel that my face reminded him of anything. So much the better. What a relief . . .

I've never understood the role of Jeannette Gaul at Le Canter. She often used to take orders and serve the customers. She would sit down at their table. She knew most of them. She introduced me to a tall dark-haired man with oriental looks, a certain Accad, the son of a local doctor, very well dressed, and who behaved as though he had studied. He was always accompanied by two friends, Godinger and Mario Bay. Sometimes they played cards and other games with older men in the small room at the back. This would go on until five o'clock in the morning. One of these players was apparently the actual owner of Le Canter. A man of about fifty with short grey hair, also very well dressed, with an austere expression and who Jeannette had told me was a "former lawyer". I remember his name: Mocellini. From time to time, he would stand up and go to join Suzanne behind the bar. On some nights, he took over from her and served the drinks himself, as though he was at home in his own apartment and all the customers were his guests. He called Jeannette "my dear" or "Death's Head" without my understanding why, and on the first occasions I came to Le Canter he looked at me somewhat suspiciously. One night, he asked me how old I was. I made myself older, I said "twenty-one". He stared at me and frowned; he did not believe me. "Are you sure you're twenty-one?" I felt more and more embarrassed and was ready to tell him my real age, but his expression suddenly lost all its sternness. He smiled at me and shrugged. "Very well, let's say you are twenty-one."

Jeannette had a soft spot for Mario Bay. He wore tinted

spectacles, but not out of affectation in the least. The light hurt his eyes. Delicate hands. To begin with, Jeannette had taken him for a pianist, one of those, she told me, who perform in concerts at the Gaveau or the Pleyel. He was about thirty, like Accad and Godinger. But if he wasn't a pianist, what did he do with his life? He and Accad were very close to Mocellini. According to Jeannette, they had worked with Mocellini when he was still a lawyer. Afterwards, they continued to work for him. Doing what? In societies, she told me. But what did that mean, "societies"? They used to invite us to their table at Le Canter, and Jeannette claimed that Accad had a crush on me. From the start, I felt that she wanted me to go out with him, perhaps in order to strengthen her ties with Mario Bay. I rather had the impression that it was Godinger who liked me. He was dark-haired like Accad, but taller. Jeannette did not know him as well as the other two. He evidently had a lot of money and a car that he always parked outside Le Canter. He lived in the hotel and he often went to Belgium.

Lapses of memory. And then details that spring to mind, details that are as specific as they are insignificant. He lived in the hotel and he often went to Belgium. The other evening, I repeated this silly sentence as though it was the refrain of a lullaby you hum in the dark to comfort yourself. And so why did Mocellini call Jeannette Death's Head? Details that obscure other, more painful ones. I remember the afternoon, a few years later, when Jeannette came to see me in Neuilly. It was two weeks after my marriage to Jean-Pierre Choureau. I've never been able to call him other than Jean-Pierre Choureau, probably because he was older than me and because he addressed me as "*vous*". She rang the bell three times, as I had asked her to do. For a second, I didn't want to answer her, but that was ridiculous, she knew my phone number and my address. She came in, slipping through the half-opened door, and it was as though she were sneaking into the apartment to burgle it. She glanced around the drawing room, the white walls, the low table, the pile of magazines, the lamp with its red shade, the portrait of Jean-Pierre Choureau's mother above the sofa. She said nothing. She nodded. She wanted to use the lavatory. She seemed amazed that Jean-Pierre Choureau and I should sleep in separate rooms. We both lay down on the bed in my room.

"So, he's a boy from a good family?" Jeannette said to me. And she burst out laughing.

I had not seen her since the hotel in rue d'Armaillé. Her laugh made me feel uncomfortable. I was afraid she might take me back in time, to the Le Canter period. Yet, when she had come to visit me the previous year in rue d'Armaillé, she had informed me she had broken up with the others.

"A real young lady's bedroom . . ."

On the chest of drawers, the photograph of Jean-Pierre Choureau in a garnet-coloured leather frame. She stood up and leant over towards it.

"He's rather a handsome guy . . . But why are you in separate bedrooms?"

Once again, she lay down beside me on the bed. Then I told her that I would prefer to see her somewhere else, not here. I was afraid she might feel awkward in Jean-Pierre Choureau's presence. And then we wouldn't be able to speak freely together.

"Are you frightened I might come to see you with the others?"

She laughed, but less openly than she had before. It's true, I was frightened, even in Neuilly, of coming across Accad. I was surprised that he hadn't discovered my whereabouts when I lived in the hotels, in rue de l'Étoile then rue d'Armaillé.

"Don't worry . . . They haven't been in Paris for a long time . . . They're in Morocco . . ."

She stroked my brow as though she wanted to soothe me.

"I imagine you haven't talked to your husband about the parties at Cabassud..."

She had not added any irony to what she had just said. On the contrary, I was struck by her sad voice. It was her own friend, Mario Bay, the guy with the tinted spectacles and the hands of a pianist, who used this word "parties" when they took us, Accad and he, to spend the night at Cabassud, an inn not far from Paris.

"It's quiet here ... It's not like Cabassud ... Do you remember?"

Details that made me want to close my eyes, as you do when the light is too bright. And yet, the other time, when we had left Guy de Vere's friends and I was coming back from Montmartre with Roland, I kept my eyes wide open. Everything was clearer, sharper, a harsh light dazzled me and eventually I grew accustomed to it. One night at Le Canter, I found myself in this same light with Jeannette at a table, near the entrance. There was no-one left apart from Mocellini and the others who were playing cards in the back room, behind the metal screen. My mother must have returned home a long time ago. I wondered whether she was worried about my absence. I almost regretted that night when she had come to collect me from the Grandes-Carrières police station. I had the feeling that from now on she would never be able to collect me again. I was too far away. A feeling of anxiety came over me that I tried to control and it prevented me from breathing. Jeannette drew her face closer to mine.

"You're very pale . . . Are you all right?"

I wanted to smile so as to reassure her, but I had the impression I was making a face.

"No . . . It's nothing . . ."

Ever since I started leaving the apartment at night, I had had brief panic attacks, or rather, "low blood pressure", as the chemist from place Blanche had said one evening when I was trying to explain to him how I was feeling. But each time I uttered a word, it seemed to me false or meaningless. Better to remain silent. A sense of emptiness suddenly came over me in the street. The first time, it was outside the tobacconist's, beyond Le Cyrano. There were a lot of people there, but that did not make me feel any better. I was about to pass out and they would continue to walk straight on without taking any notice of me. Low blood pressure. Power cut. I had to take a hold of myself in order to reconnect the wires. On that evening, I had gone into the tobacconist's and I had asked for stamps, postcards, a ball-point pen and a pack of cigarettes. I had sat down at the counter. I had taken a postcard and started to write. "Just wait a little bit longer. I think things will be better." I had lit a cigarette and stuck a stamp on the card. But who to send it to? I should have liked to write a few words on each of the postcards, some re-assuring words: "The weather's fine, I'm having a lovely holiday, I hope everything's fine with you too. See you soon. Love." I'm sitting at the terrace of a café very early in the morning, beside the sea. And I'm writing postcards to friends.

"How are you feeling? Any better?" Jeannette said to me. Her face was even closer to mine.

"Would you like us to go outside for some air?"

The street had never seemed to me to be so deserted and silent. It was lit by lamplights from another age. And to think that you only had to climb the hill to find, a few hundred metres away, the Saturday evening crowd, the neon signs that advertise "The loveliest nudes in the world" and the tourist buses out-side the Moulin-Rouge . . . I was frightened by all this bustling activity. I said to Jeannette:

"We could stop halfway up . . ."

We had walked as far as where the lights began, the

crossroads at the end of rue Notre-Dame-de-Lorette. But we turned around and followed the gradient of the road in the opposite direction. I felt gradually more relieved as I went down this hill, on the shady side. You just had to let yourself go. Jeannette was clutching my arm. We had almost reached the bottom of the hill, at the intersection with La Tour-des-Dames. She said to me:

"Wouldn't you like us to have a little snow?"

I didn't understand the precise meaning of this sentence, but the word "snow" struck me. I had the impression that at any moment it was about to fall and make the silence all around us even deeper. All we would hear would be the crunch of our footsteps in the snow. A clock chimed somewhere and, I don't know why, I thought it was calling people to midnight mass. Jeannette was guiding me. I let myself be swept along. We were walking along rue d'Aumale where all the buildings were darkened. It was as though they formed one single black frontage on each side, from one end of the street to the other.

"Come to my room . . . we'll have a little snow . . ."

As soon as we arrived, I would ask her what that meant: have a little snow. It felt colder because of these black façades. Was I in a dream to be hearing the echo of our footsteps so clearly?

Afterwards, I often took the same route, alone or with her. I used to go and meet her in her room during the daytime or else I would spend the night there when we stayed too late at Le Canter. It was in a hotel in rue Laferrière, a street that has a sharp bend in it and where you feel removed from everything, in the area where the gradient starts to rise. A lift with a lattice gate. It went up slowly. She lived on the top floor, or higher still. Perhaps the lift wasn't going to stop. She whispered in my ear:

"You'll see . . . it'll be great . . . we'll have a little snow . . ."

Her hands were quivering. In the dim light of the corridor, she was so anxious that she wasn't able to get the key into the lock.

"Go on . . . you try . . . I can't manage it . . ."

Her voice was more and more halting. She had dropped the key. I bent down to grope around for it. I succeeded in sliding it into the lock. The light was on, a yellow light that fell from the ceiling. The bed was unmade, the curtains drawn. She sat down on the edge of the bed and she rummaged in the drawer of the bedside table. From it, she took a small metal box. She told me to inhale this white powder that she called "snow". After a while, it gave me a sense of freshness and lightness. I felt certain that the anxiety and the feeling of emptiness that came over me in the street would never return. Ever since the chemist in place Blanche had talked to me about low blood pressure, I thought I needed to brace myself, to struggle with myself, to try to control myself. There's nothing we can do, we've been brought up the hard way. Sink or swim. If I fell, others would continue to walk along boulevard de Clichy. I shouldn't have any illusions. But, from now on, that would change. What's more, the streets and the frontiers of the neighbourhood suddenly seemed to me to be too narrow.

A stationer's and bookseller's shop on boulevard de Clichy stayed open until one o'clock in the morning. Mattei. A simple name on the shop front. The name of the owner? I never dared ask this dark-haired man who wore a moustache and a Prince-of-Wales-check jacket and who was always sitting behind his desk, reading. Every time customers bought postcards or a pad of writing paper, they interrupted his reading. At the time I used to come, there were hardly any customers, except occasionally a few people who were leaving Minuit Chansons next door. Usually, we were alone in the bookshop, he and I. The same books were always displayed in the shop window and I soon realised that they were science fiction. He had recommended that I read them. I remember the titles of some of them: *A*

Pebble in the Sky. Stowaway to Mars. Vandals of the Void. I have only kept one of them: *The Dreaming Jewels.*

On the right, on the shelves by the window, there were second-hand books devoted to astronomy. I picked out one that had an orange jacket that was half-torn: *A Voyage into Space.* I still have that too. On the Saturday evening when I wanted to buy it, I was the only customer in the bookshop and you could barely hear the din from the boulevard. On the other side of the window, a few neon signs could be seen, even the blue and white one with "The Loveliest nudes in the world", but they seemed so far away . . . I didn't dare disturb this man who was sitting there reading, his head bent forward. I stood there in silence for ten minutes or so before he turned to me. I handed him the book. He smiled: "Very good, that. Very good . . . *A Voyage into Space* . . ." I got ready to pay him the price of the book, but he raised his arm: "No . . . no . . . I'm giving it to you . . . And I wish you a good journey . . ."

Yes, this bookshop was not merely a refuge but also a stage in my life. I often stayed there until closing time. There was a chair placed near the shelves, or rather a large stool. I would sit there, leafing through the books and the illustrated titles. I wondered whether he was aware of my presence. After a few days, without interrupting his reading, he would make a remark to me, always the same one: "So, did you find what you're looking for?" Later on, someone informed me with great confidence that the only thing one can never remember is the timbre of people's voices. Yet, even today, during my sleepless nights, I can hear the voice with its Parisian accent – that of the districts with steep, hilly streets – saying to me: "So, did you find what you're looking for?" And this remark has lost none of its kindness and its mystery.

In the evening, on leaving the bookshop, I was amazed to find myself back on boulevard de Clichy. I didn't much feel like walking down to Le Canter. My feet were luring me upwards. I now experienced pleasure in climbing gradients or staircases. I counted every step. By the time I reached the number 30, I knew that I was safe. Much later, Guy de Vere made me read *Lost Horizon*, the story of people who climb the mountains of Tibet to the monastery of Shangri-La in order to learn the secrets of life and of wisdom. But there's no point in going so far. I remembered my night-time walks. For me, Montmartre was Tibet. All I needed was the gradient of rue Caulaincourt. Up there, outside the Château des Brouillards, I breathed for the first time in my life. One day, at dawn, I ran away from Le Canter where

I was with Jeannette. We were waiting for Accad and Mario Bay, who wanted to take us to Cabassud together with Godinger and another girl. I felt suffocated. I invented an excuse to go and get some air. I started to run. All the neon signs were lit up on the square, even those of the Moulin-Rouge. I allowed myself to be swept along by a sense of intoxication that alcohol or snow would never have given me. I walked up the hill as far as the Château des Brouillards. I had made up my mind never to see the gang from Le Canter again. Later on, I used to feel the same exhilaration each time I broke up with someone. I wasn't truly myself except at the moment I was running away. My only good memories are memories of flight or escape. But life always got the upper hand. When I reached allée des Brouillards, I felt sure that someone had arranged to meet me around here and that this would be a new start for me. There is a street, a little higher up, to which I should like to return some day. I followed it that morning. It was there that the meeting would take place. But I didn't know the number of the building. No matter. I waited for a sign that would tell me. Over there, the street emerged into the open sky, as though it were leading to the edge of a cliff. I walked on with that feeling of lightness that sometimes comes over one in dreams. You're no longer afraid of anything, all the dangers are absurd. If things get really bad, all you have to do is wake up. You are invincible. I walked, eager to arrive at the end, where there would be nothing but the blue of the sky and open space. What word would convey my state of mind? I only have a very limited vocabulary. Intoxication? Ecstasy? Rapture? In any case, this street was familiar to me. It seemed to me that I had walked along it in the past. I would soon reach the edge of the cliff and I would throw myself into the void. What joy to float in the air and to experience at last that sense of weightlessness that I had always yearned. I remember that morning with such great clarity, that street and the sky at the very end . . .

And then life continued, with its ups and downs. One day when I was feeling low, on the cover of the book that Guy de Vere had lent me, *Louise du Néant*, I substituted in ballpoint pen the first name with my own. *Jacqueline du Néant*.

THAT EVENING, IT WAS AS THOUGH WE WERE TABLE-
tapping. We were gathered together in Guy de Vere's office
and he had switched off the light. Or else, quite simply, it was
a power cut. We could hear his voice in the darkness. He was
reciting a passage of text to us which he would otherwise have
read in the light. But no, I'm being unfair, Guy de Vere would
have been shocked to hear me talking about "table-tapping" in
connection with him. He was better than that. He would have
said to me in a tone of slight reproof: "Come now, Roland . . ."

He lit the candles in a candelabrum on the mantelpiece and
then he sat down again behind his desk. We were seated on
chairs, facing him, this girl, myself and a couple in their forties,
both very neatly dressed and bourgeois in appearance, whom I
was meeting here for the first time.

I looked over at her and our eyes met. Guy de Vere was still talking, slightly hunched forward, but speaking very naturally, sounding almost as though he were having an everyday conversation. At each meeting, he read a passage of text which he photocopied for us later on. I've kept the photocopy for that particular evening. I had a reference point. She had given me her phone number and I had written it at the bottom of the sheet, in red ballpoint pen.

"Maximum concentration is obtained lying down, with one's eyes closed. At the slightest outside distraction, dispersion and diffusion begin. Standing up, the legs take away some of the strength. Open eyes reduce concentration."

I had difficulty controlling a fit of the giggles and I remember it all the more because this had never happened to me until then. But the candlelight gave this reading far too solemn an air. Our eyes met frequently. It was clear that she had no desire to laugh. On the contrary, she seemed very respectful, and even anxious about not understanding what the words meant. She eventually communicated this serious-mindedness to me. I felt almost ashamed at my first reaction. I hardly dared think of the embarrassment I would have created had I burst out laughing. And in her expression, I thought I saw a sort of call for help, a questioning look. Am I worthy to be among you? Guy de Vere's fingers were joined as if in prayer. His voice had taken on a more solemn tone and he was staring at her as though he were addressing her alone. This petrified her. Perhaps she was frightened that he might ask her an unexpected question, of the kind: "And what about you, I'd really like to know your opinion on the matter."

The light came back on. We remained in the study for a few moments longer, which was unusual. The meetings had always taken place in the drawing room where about ten people were gathered together. That particular evening, there were only four of us and de Vere had probably chosen to invite us to his study because we were so few. And this was arranged through a simple meeting, without the usual invitation that you would receive at your home or be given at the Véga bookshop if you were a regular customer. As with a number of photocopies, I've kept a few of these invitations, and I came across one of them yesterday:

My dear Roland,

Guy de Vere

would be glad to welcome you

on Thursday, 16th January at 8.00 p.m.

at 5 square Lowendal (XVe)

2nd block to the left

3rd floor left

The white invitation card, always in the same format, with its ornate lettering, might have been informing one of a social gathering, a cocktail or birthday party.

That evening he accompanied us to the door of the apartment. Guy de Vere and the couple coming for the first time were twenty years or so older than either of us. Since the lift was too narrow for four people, she and I walked down the stairs.

A private road lined with identical buildings with beige- and brick-coloured frontages. The same wrought-iron gates with lanterns above them. The same rows of windows. Once past the entrance gate, we found ourselves in the rue Alexandre-Cabanel gardens. I was determined to write down this name because it was there that our paths crossed. We stood motionless for a moment in the middle of this square searching for something to say. It was I who broke the silence.

"Do you live in the neighbourhood?"

"No, near the Étoile."

I searched for an excuse not to leave her immediately. "We could go together for part of the way."

We walked beneath the viaduct, the length of boulevard de Grenelle. She had suggested to me that we follow this part of the elevated métro line that leads to the Étoile on foot. If she felt tired, she could always travel the rest of the way by métro. It must have been a Sunday evening or a holiday. There was no traffic and all the cafés were closed. In any case, as I recall, we were in a deserted city that night. When I think of it now, our encounter strikes me as the encounter of two people who had no anchorage in life. I think that we were both alone in the world.

"Have you known Guy de Vere for long?" I asked her.

"No, I met him through a friend at the beginning of the year. And you?"

"I met him through the Véga bookshop."

She didn't know of the existence of this bookshop on boulevard Saint-Germain where the window displayed a sign in blue letters: *Orientalism and Comparative Religions*. It was there I had first heard of Guy de Vere. One evening, the bookseller had given me one of the invitation cards and told me that I could attend the meeting. "It's perfect for people like you." I should have liked to ask him what he meant by "people like you". He looked at me with a degree of kindliness and it was not intended in any derogatory way. He even suggested "recommending" me to this Guy de Vere.

"And is it nice, the Véga bookshop?"

She asked me this question in a mocking tone of voice. But it may have been her Parisian accent that gave me this impression.

"You find lots of interesting books there. I'll take you there."

I wanted to know what books she read and what had attracted her to Guy de Vere's gatherings. The first book that de Vere had recommended to her was *Lost Horizon*. She had read it with a great deal of care. At the previous meeting, she had arrived earlier than the others, and de Vere had asked her into his study. He was searching the shelves of his library, which took up two entire walls, for another book to lend her. After a short while, as if an idea had suddenly come to mind, he had made his way towards his study and had picked up a book that was lying among the disorderly piles of files and letters. He had said to her: "You can read this. I'd be curious to know what you think of it." She had been very nervous. De Vere always spoke to other people as though they were as intelligent and as cultured as he was. For how long? In the end, he would realise that we were not on his level. The title of the book he had given her that evening was: *Louise du Néant*. No, I didn't know it. It was the story of the life of Louise du Néant, a nun, together with all the letters she had written. She did not read the book in sequence, she opened it at random. Certain pages had impressed her a great deal. Even more than *Lost Horizon*. Before knowing de Vere, she had read science-fiction novels such as *The Dreaming Jewels*. And books on astronomy. What a coincidence . . . I, too, liked astronomy very much.

At Bir-Hakeim station, I wondered whether she was going to take the métro or whether she wanted to go on walking and cross over the Seine. Above us, at regular intervals, could be heard the din of the trains. We stepped onto the bridge.

"I live near the Étoile too," I told her. "Possibly not very far from where you live."

She hesitated. She probably wanted to tell me something that embarrassed her.

"Actually, I'm married . . . I live with my husband in Neuilly . . ."

Anyone would think she had confessed a crime to me.

"And have you been married for long?"

"No. Not very long . . . since April last year . . ."

We were walking again. We had reached the middle of the bridge, level with the steps that lead to allée des Cygnes. She set off down the steps and I followed her. She walked down them at a steady pace, as though she was going to a rendezvous. And she spoke to me in an increasingly rapid tone of voice.

"At a certain point, I was looking for work . . . I came across an advertisement . . . It was for a temporary secretary . . ."

Once at the bottom, we walked along the allée des Cygnes. On either side were the Seine and the lights of the embankment. I felt as though I was on the promenade deck of a ship that had run aground in the middle of the night.

"At the office, a man gave me work to do . . . He was kind to me . . . He was older . . . After a certain time, he wanted to get married . . ."

It was as though she was trying to justify herself to a childhood friend whom she had not been in touch with for a long time, and whom she had come across by chance in the street.

"But what about you, were you glad to get married?"

She shrugged, as if I had said something absurd. At any moment, I expected her to say: "But come on now, you who know me so well . . ."

I must, after all, have known her in a previous life.

"He always said that he wanted to do what was best for me ... It's true ... He does want what is best for me ... He behaves rather as though he were my father . . ."

I thought that she was expecting some advice from me. She probably wasn't used to confiding in people.

"And doesn't he ever come with you to the meetings?"

"No. He has too much work."

She had met de Vere through a childhood friend of her husband's. He had brought de Vere to dinner at their home in Neuilly. She frowned as she gave me all these details, as though she was frightened of forgetting any of them, even the most insignificant one.

We were at the end of the pathway, opposite the statue of Liberty. A bench on the right. I don't know which of us took the initiative to sit down there, or perhaps we both had the idea at the same time. I asked her whether she should not go home. This was the third or fourth occasion that she had attended Guy de Vere's meetings, and that she had found herself by the stairs to Cambronne station at about eleven o'clock at night. And each time she felt a kind of despondency at the prospect of returning to Neuilly. So she was doomed from now on to take the same métro line for evermore. Change at Étoile. Get off at Sablons...

I felt the touch of her shoulder against mine. She told me that after this dinner party where she had met Guy de Vere for the first time he had invited her to a lecture he was giving at a small theatre near the Odéon. On that particular day, it was to do with the "dark South" and the "green light". On leaving the hall, she had wandered aimlessly around the neighbourhood. She was floating in that green and limpid light that Guy de Vere spoke about. Five o'clock in the afternoon. There was a lot of traffic on the boulevard and at the Odéon crossroads people were jostling her because she was walking against the flow and did not wish to go down the stairs to the métro station with them. An empty street rose gently towards the Luxembourg Gardens. And there, halfway up the slope, she had walked into a café, on the corner of a building: Le Condé. "Do you know Le Condé?" All of a sudden she started to call me "*tu*". No, I didn't know Le Condé. To tell the truth, I didn't much care for this Écoles area. It reminded me of my childhood, the dormitories of a *lycée* that I had been expelled from, and a university restaurant, near rue Dauphine, that I was obliged to go to, using a forged student card. I was starving. Afterwards, she often took refuge in Le Condé. She had soon got to know most of the regulars, in particular two writers: a certain Maurice Raphaël, and Arthur Adamov. Had I heard of them? Yes. I knew who Adamov was. I had even seen him, on several occasions, near Saint-Julien-le-Pauvre. An anxious look on his face. I would even say horror-stricken. He was walking about wearing only sandals on his feet. She had not read any of Adamov's books. At Le Condé, he sometimes asked her to accompany him to his hotel because he was frightened of walking on his own at night. Ever since she had started going to Le Condé, the others had given her a nickname. Her name was Jacqueline, but they called her Louki. If I wanted, she would introduce me to Adamov and the others. And also Jimmy Campbell, an English singer. And a Tunisian friend, Ali Cherif. We could meet at Le Condé during the day. She also used to go there in the evening, when her husband was out. He would often come home very late from his work. She looked up at me and, after a moment's hesitation, she told me that each time it was a little harder for her to return to her husband in Neuilly. She seemed preoccupied and she didn't utter another word.

It was time for the last métro. We were alone in the carriage. Before changing trains at Étoile, she gave me her phone number.

*

Even today, in the evenings, I occasionally hear a voice calling me by my first name, in the street. A husky voice. There's a slight drawl to the syllables and I recognise it immediately: Louki's voice. I turn around, but there's no-one there. Not just in the evening, but in the midst of those summer afternoons when you're no longer quite sure what year you're in. Everything will begin again as before. The same days, the same nights, the same places, the same encounters. The Eternal Recurrence.

I often hear the voice in my dreams. Everything is so precise – to the slightest detail – that I ask myself, on waking up, how this is possible. The other night, I dreamt that I was leaving Guy de Vere's building, at the same time that we had left, Louki and I, on the first occasion. I looked at my watch. Eleven o'clock at night. At one of the ground-floor windows, there was some ivy. I walked through the gate and I was crossing square Cambronne in the direction of the overhead railway when I heard Louki's voice. She called me: "Roland . . ." Twice. I sensed some irony in her voice. She used to make fun of my first name, to begin with, a first name that was not mine. I had chosen it to simplify matters, an all-purpose first name, which could also be used as a surname. It was convenient, Roland. And above all, so French. My real name was too exotic. In those days, I avoided drawing attention to myself. "Roland . . ." I turned around. No-one. I was in the middle of the square, like the first time when we didn't know what to say to each other. On waking up, I decided to go to Guy de Vere's former address to discover whether there really was ivy at the ground-floor window. I took the métro as far as Cambronne. It was the line Louki took when she was still going back to her husband in Neuilly. I would accompany her and we often got off at Argentine station, near the hotel where I lived. On each occasion, she would happily have stayed in my room all night, but she would make a final effort and return to Neuilly . . . And then, one night, she did stay with me, at Argentine.

I felt a strange sensation walking to square Cambronne in the morning, because it was always night-time when we used to go to Guy de Vere's. I pushed open the gate and I told myself that I hadn't the slightest chance of meeting him after all this time. No longer a Véga bookshop on boulevard Saint-Germain and no longer a Guy de Vere in Paris. And no more Louki. But at the ground-floor window, the ivy was there, as in my dream. This caused me great distress. The other night, was it really a dream? I stood stock-still for a moment gazing at the window.

I hoped to hear Louki's voice. She would call to me once more. No. Nothing. Silence. But I didn't have any sense that time had passed since the Guy de Vere period. On the contrary, he was frozen in a sort of eternity. I remembered the piece I was trying to write when I had known Louki. I had entitled it "The Neutral Zones". Intermediary zones existed in Paris, no-man's-lands where you were on the fringes of everything, in transit, or even suspended. You enjoyed a degree of immunity there. I could have called them free zones, but neutral zones was more exact. One evening, at Le Condé, I had asked Maurice Raphaël's opinion, since he was a writer. He had shrugged his shoulders and had given me a mocking smile: "It's up to you to find out, old boy . . . I don't really understand what you're driving at . . . Let's say 'neutral' and not discuss it anymore . . ." Square Cambronne and the neighbourhood between Ségur and Dupleix, all those roads that lead to the overhead railway bridges belong to a neutral zone, and it would not have been a mere coincidence were I to have met Louki there.

I've lost that bit of text. Five pages that I had typed out on the machine that Zacharias, a customer at Le Condé, had lent me. I had written as a dedication: "For Louki of the neutral zones". I don't know what she thought of this piece of work.

I don't believe she ever read it right through. It was rather an unappealing passage, a listing by arrondissements of the names of the streets that circumscribed these neutral zones. Occasionally, a cluster of houses, or else a much broader expanse. One afternoon when we were both at Le Condé, she had just read the dedication and she had said to me: "You know, Roland, we could go and spend a week in each of the areas you mention..."

Rue d'Argentine, where I rented a hotel room, was very much in a neutral zone. Who could have come to look for me there? The rare people I did come across there must have been dead as far as the registry office was concerned. One day, leafing through a newspaper, I came across the heading "legal publications" over a paragraph entitled: "Declaration of absence". A certain Tarride had not returned to his home address nor had anyone had news of him for thirty years, and the county court had declared him "missing". I had shown this notification to Louki. We were in my room in rue d'Argentine. I had told her that I was sure this man lived in the street, along with dozens of others who had also been declared "missing". Furthermore, the buildings adjoining my hotel all displayed notices advertising "furnished apartments". Areas that people pass through, where no-one asked you for identity papers and where you could hide. That particular day, we had been celebrating La Houpa's birthday with the others, at Le Condé. They had plied us with drink. When we returned to the room, we were slightly drunk. I opened the window. I shouted out as loudly as possible: "Tarride! Tarride! . . ." The street was deserted and this name made a strange echoing sound. I even had the impression that the echo was calling back to us. Louki came and stood beside me and she also yelled: "Tarride! . . . Tarride! . . ." A childish joke that made us laugh. But in the end I began to believe that this man was going to make an appearance and we would bring back to life all the missing people who haunted this street. After a short while, the nightwatchman from the hotel came and knocked on our door. In a voice from beyond the grave, he said: "A little silence, please." We heard his heavy footsteps going down the stairs. I concluded from this that he himself was a missing person like the man called Tarride and all those who were hiding in furnished rooms in rue d'Argentine.

I thought of this every time I walked along this street to return to my room. Louki had told me that she, too, before getting married, had lived in two hotels in this neighbourhood, slightly further to the north, in rue d'Armaillé, and then rue de l'Étoile. In those days, we must have passed each other by without seeing one another.

I remember the evening when she decided not to return to her husband anymore. That day, at Le Condé, she had introduced me to Adamov and Ali Cherif. I was carrying the typewriter that Zacharias had lent me. I intended to start "The Neutral Zones".

I had put the machine down on the little pitch pine table in the room. I already had the first sentence in mind: "The neutral zones have this advantage at least: they are merely a starting point and, sooner or later, you leave them." I knew that with the typewriter in front of me everything would be far less simple. I would probably have to cross out this first sentence. And the next one. And yet, I felt full of courage.

She was due to return to Neuilly for dinner, but at eight o'clock she was still stretched out on the bed. She had not switched on the bedside light. Eventually, I reminded her of the time.

"Time for what?"

From the tone of her voice, I realised that she would never take the métro to alight at Sablons station again. A long silence between us. I sat down at the typewriter and I tapped away on the keys.

"We could go to the cinema," she said to me. "That would pass the time."

You only had to cross the avenue de la Grande-Armée and you came to the Studio Obligado. Neither of us had paid attention to the film that evening. I believe the audience was very sparse. A few people that a court had declared "missing" for a long time? And what about us, who were we? I glanced at her from time to time. She was not looking at the screen, her head was leaning forward and she seemed to be lost in thought. I was afraid she might get to her feet and go back to Neuilly. But no. She stayed until the end of the film.

When we left the Studio Obligado, she seemed relieved. She told me that it was now too late for her to return to her husband's home. He had invited a few friends of his to dinner that evening. Well, it was over. There would never be any dinner party at Neuilly again.

We did not return to the room immediately. We walked around for a long time in this neutral zone where each of us had sheltered at different periods. She wanted to show me the hotels in which she had lived, in rue d'Armaillé and rue de l'Étoile. I try to remember what she told me that night. It was confused. Nothing but snatches. And it's too late now to find out the details that are missing or that I may have forgotten. She had left her mother, and the neighbourhood in which she had lived with her, when she was very young. Her mother was dead. There was one friend of hers who remained from that period whom she saw from time to time, a certain Jeannette Gaul. On two or three occasions, we had had dinner with Jeannette Gaul in a run-down restaurant near my hotel. A blonde with green eyes. Louki had told me that she was known as Death's Head on account of her emaciated face that contrasted with a generously curvaceous body. Later on, Jeannette Gaul called on her at the hotel in rue Cels and I should have asked myself questions the day that I caught them unawares in the bedroom where a smell of ether lingered. And then one breezy, sunny afternoon on the embankment, opposite Notre-Dame . . . I was looking at books in the *bouquinistes'* green boxes while waiting for both of them. Jeannette Gaul had said that she had an appointment in rue des Grands-Degrés with someone who was going to bring her "a little snow" . . . That made her smile, the word "snow", considering we were in the month of July . . . In one of the *bouquinistes'* green boxes, I happened on a paperback the title of which was

Le Bel Été. Yes, it was a beautiful summer because to me it seemed eternal. And I saw them, all of a sudden, on the other pavement of the embankment. They were coming back from rue des Grands-Degrés. Louki waved at me. They were walking towards me in the sun and the silence. That is how they often appear to me in my dreams, both of them, near Saint-Julien-le-Pauvre . . . That afternoon, I believe I was happy.

I did not understand why Jeannette Gaul had been given the nickname Death's Head. Because of her high cheekbones and her slanting eyes? Yet there was nothing about her face that suggested death. She was still at that period when youth outweighs everything else. Nothing – neither the sleepless nights, nor the snow, as she used to call it – left the slightest mark on her. For how long? I should have been wary of her. Louki did not bring her to Le Condé or to Guy de Vere's gatherings; it was as if the girl represented her dark side. I only once heard them talk about their common past in my presence, and then only hesitantly. I had the impression that they shared secrets. One day when I was coming out of Mabillon métro station with Louki – a November day at about six o'clock in the evening, when night had already fallen – she recognised someone sitting at a table on the other side of the large window at

La Pergola. She recoiled slightly. A man of about fifty, with a stern expression and dark, plastered-down hair. He was almost facing us and he, too, may have seen us. But I think he was talking to someone sitting next to him. She took my arm and dragged me away to the other side of rue du Four. She told me that she had known this guy two years ago with Jeannette Gaul and that he ran a restaurant in the 9th arrondissement. She had certainly not expected to see him here, on the Left Bank. She seemed anxious. She had used the words "Left Bank" as though the Seine were a demarcation line that separated two foreign cities from one another, a sort of iron curtain. And the man at La Pergola had succeeded in crossing this frontier. His presence there, at the Mabillon crossroads, genuinely bothered her. I asked her his name. Mocellini. And why she wanted to avoid him. She did not give me a straightforward reply. It was just that the guy brought back bad memories. When she broke up with people, it was for good, they were dead as far as she was concerned. If this man was still alive and there was a chance she might come across him, then it was better to change neighbourhoods.

I reassured her. La Pergola was not like other cafés, and its rather sleazy clientele was not comparable in any way to the studious, bohemian district in which we were walking. Had she told me that she had known this Mocellini in the 9th arrondissement? Well, exactly, La Pergola was a kind of annexe of Pigalle in Saint-Germain-des-Prés, without anyone quite understanding why. You only had to walk on the other pavement and avoid La Pergola. No need to change neighbourhoods.

I should have insisted on her telling me more about this, but I knew roughly what her answer would be, always supposing she was willing to answer me . . . in my childhood and teenage years I had met so many Mocellinis, characters whom you later wonder about, about what sort of racket they were involved in . . . Had I not frequently seen my father in the company of such people? After all these years, I could make enquiries about the man called Mocellini. But what was the point? I would not learn anything more about Louki that I didn't know already or that I had not guessed. Are we really responsible for hangers-on whom we have not chosen to know and whom we encounter in our early life? Am I responsible for my father and for all those shadowy people who spoke to him in hushed voices in hotel foyers or the backrooms of cafés and who carried suitcases the contents of which would never be revealed to me? That evening, after this unfortunate encounter, we were walking along boulevard Saint-Germain. When we entered the Véga bookshop, she seemed relieved. She had a list of some books that Guy de Vere had recommended to her. I've kept that list. He gave it to everyone who took part in his meetings. "You're not obliged to read them all at once," he used to say. "Instead, choose just one book and read a page from it every night, before you go to sleep."

> L'Alter Ego céleste
> L'Ami de Dieu dans l'Oberland
> Chant de la Perle
> La Colonne de l'Aurore
> Les Douze Sauveurs du Trésor de lumière
> Organes ou centres subtils
> La Roseraie du mystère
> La Septième Vallée

Small booklets with pale green covers. To begin with, we used to read from them aloud, Louki and I, in my room in rue d'Argentine. It was a sort of discipline, whenever we were in low spirits. I don't believe we read these works in the same way. She hoped to discover a meaning to life from them, whereas it was the sound of the words and the music of the sentences that appealed to me. That evening, at the Véga bookshop, I think she had forgotten the man known as Mocellini and all the bad memories that he aroused. Today, I realise that it was not merely a course of action that she was looking for in reading these pale green booklets and the biography of Louise du Néant. She wanted to escape, to run ever further away, to make a sudden break from day-to-day life, so that she could breathe the fresh air. And then there was also that panic-stricken fear, from time to time, at the thought that the hangers-on you have left behind can come back and find you and ask you for explanations. You had to hide to escape these blackmailers, hoping that one day you would be beyond their reach for good. Up there, in the air of the mountain crests. Or in the sea air. I could understand this very well. I, too, still carried around bad memories and the nightmare figures of my childhood and I planned to give them the two fingers once and for all.

I told her that it was absurd to swap pavements. In the end, I persuaded her. From then on, whenever we came out of Mabillon métro station, we no longer avoided La Pergola. One evening, I even dragged her inside this café. We were standing by the bar and we were ready and waiting for Mocellini. And all the other shadows of the past. With me, she feared nothing. No better method than looking straight into the eyes of ghosts to make them disappear. I believe she was regaining her confidence and that she would not even have reacted had Mocellini appeared. I had advised her to say to him in a firm voice the phrase that I used in this kind of situation: "No, monsieur . . . It's not me . . . I'm sorry . . . You've made a mistake . . ."

We waited for Mocellini that evening in vain. And we never did see him again through the window.

That February when she didn't go home to her husband, it snowed a great deal and in rue d'Argentine we had the feeling that we were marooned in a mountain-top hotel. I realised that it was difficult to live in a neutral zone. It was actually better to be closer to the centre. The strangest thing about this rue d'Argentine – though I had made a list of a few other Paris streets that resembled it – was that it did not correspond to the arrondissement to which it belonged. It did not correspond to anything, it was disconnected from everything. With this layer of snow, it led into empty space on either side. I must find the list of streets that are not only neutral zones, but are black holes within Paris. Or rather, fragments of that dark matter that occurs in astronomy, a matter that makes everything invisible and which would resist even ultra-violet, infra-red or X-rays. Yes, in the long run, we risk being sucked up by the dark matter.

She did not want to stay in a neighbourhood that was too close to her husband's home. Barely two métro stations away. She was looking for a hotel on the Left Bank in the vicinity of Le Condé or Guy de Vere's apartment. In that way, she would be able to walk there. As for me, I was frightened of returning from the other side of the Seine to this 6th arrondissement of my childhood. So many painful memories . . . But there's no point in talking about them since this arrondissement no longer exists nowadays except for those who own luxury shops there and the wealthy foreigners who buy apartments there . . . At the time, I still found traces of my childhood: the run-down hotels on rue Dauphine, the place where catechism classes used to take place, the café at the Odéon crossroads where a few deserters from the American bases used to traffic drugs, the dark staircase of the Vert-Galant, and that scrawl on the grimy wall on rue Mazar-ine, which I read every time I went to school: NEVER WORK.

When she rented a room a little further south, towards Mont-parnasse, I remained in the Étoile district. I wanted to avoid encountering any ghosts on the Left Bank. Apart from in my old haunts, Le Condé and the Véga Bookshop, I preferred not to linger too much around my former neighbourhood.

And then some money had to be found. She had sold a fur coat that was probably a present from her husband. All she had left was a flimsy raincoat with which to brave the winter. She used to read the small ads as she had done just before she got married. And from time to time, she would go and visit a garage owner in Auteuil, a former friend of her mother's, who came to her aid. I scarcely dare confess to the type of work I was involved in myself. But why hide the truth?

A certain Béraud-Bedoin lived in the block of houses in which my hotel was situated. 8 rue de Saigon, to be precise. A furnished room. I came across him frequently and I no longer remember the first time we entered into conversation. A shifty sort of character with wavy hair, always dressed somewhat ostentatiously and who affected a social nonchalance. I was sitting opposite him, at a table in the café-cum-restaurant on rue d'Argentine, one afternoon during the winter that snow fell over Paris. When he asked me the usual question, "And what about you, what do you do with your life?", I had mentioned to him that I wanted to "write". I had not quite grasped what the name of Béraud-Bedoin's company was. That afternoon, I had accompanied him to his "office" – "very near here", he had told me. Our footsteps left traces in the snow. All we had to do was walk straight ahead as far as rue de Chalgrin. I have since consulted an old directory for that year to find out where exactly this Béraud-Bedoin "worked". Sometimes, we remember certain epi- sodes of our life and we need proof to be quite sure we have not been dreaming. 14 rue de Chalgrin. "Éditions commerciales de France". It must have been there. Nowadays, I don't have the courage to go along and look around the building. I am too old. He had not asked me into his office that day, but we had met the following day at the same time, at the same café. He offered me a job. It was a matter of writing several pamphlets to do with companies or organisations for which he was more or less the salesman or publicity agent, and which were to be printed by his publishing firm. He would pay me what in those days was five thousand francs. He would be named as author of the texts. I would work as his ghost-writer. He would provide me with all the documentation. That is how I came to work on ten or so short works, *Les Eaux minérales de La Bourboule*, *Le Tourisme en Côte d'Émeraude*, *Histoire des hôtels et des casinos de Bagnoles-de-l'Orne*, and on monographs devoted to the Jordaan,

Seligmann, Mirabaud and Demachy banks. Each time I sat down at my desk, I was afraid of falling asleep out of boredom. But it was fairly straightforward, merely a matter of restructuring Béraud-Bedoin's notes. I had been surprised the first time he had taken me to the headquarters of Éditions commerciales de France: a ground-floor room with no window, but at the age I was, you don't ask yourself many questions. You trust in life. Two or three months later, I had not heard a word from my publisher. He had only given me half of the promised amount and that was more than enough for me. One day – and why not tomorrow if I feel strong enough – I should perhaps go on a pilgrimage to rue de Saigon and rue de Chalgrin, a neutral zone into which Béraud-Bedoin and Éditions commerciales de France vanished with that winter's snow. But no, on further consideration, I really don't feel up to it. I even wonder whether these streets still exist and whether they haven't been absorbed once and for all by dark matter.

On a spring evening I prefer to go up the Champs-Élysées on foot. The avenue is no longer what it used to be, but at night one can still imagine it as it once was. Perhaps, on the Champs-Élysées, I will hear your voice calling me by my first name . . .

On the day you sold the fur coat and the cabochon emerald, I still had about two thousand francs of Béraud-Bedoin's money. We were rich. The future was ours. That evening, you were kind enough to come and meet me in the Étoile district. It was summer, the same summer when we had met on the embankment with Death's Head and I saw you both coming towards me. We went to the restaurant on the corner of rue François I and rue Marbeuf. They had set out tables on the pavement. It was still daylight. There was no longer any traffic and we could hear the murmur of voices and the sound of footsteps. At about ten o'clock, as we were walking down the Champs-Élysées, I wondered whether darkness would ever fall and whether we would stay up all night, as they do in Russia and the northern countries. We were walking without any precise aim, we had the entire night ahead of us. There were still glimmers of sunlight beneath the arcades of rue de Rivoli. It was early summer and we were going to go away soon. Where? We didn't yet know. Possibly to Majorca or Mexico. Perhaps to London or to Rome. The places were of no importance, they all merged together. The only purpose of our journey was to go to "the heart of the summer", to where time stops and the hands of the clock are set forever at noon.

At Palais-Royal, night had fallen. We stopped for a moment outside Le Ruc-Univers before continuing our walk. A dog followed us along rue de Rivoli as far as Saint-Paul. Then it went into the church. We didn't feel in the least tired, and Louki told me that she could walk all night. We crossed a neutral zone just before the Arsenal, a few deserted streets in which we wondered whether anyone lived. On the first floor of a building, we noticed two large illuminated windows. We sat down on a bench opposite them, and we could not stop ourselves gazing at these windows. It was the lamp with the red shade, at the very back of the room, that was casting this muted light. We could make out a mirror with a gilt frame on the left-hand wall. The other walls were bare. I was expecting that a figure would glide past the windows, but no, there was nobody, apparently, in this room and we didn't know whether it was a sitting room or a bedroom.

"We should ring at the door of the apartment," Louki said to me. "I'm sure that someone's waiting for us."

The bench was in the middle of a kind of island that formed the junction of two streets. Years later, I was in a taxi passing by the Arsenal, in the direction of the embankment. I asked the driver to stop. I wanted to find the bench and the building. I was hoping that the two first-floor windows would still be lit up, after all this time. But I almost got lost in the various small streets that led to the walls of the Célestins barracks. That night, I had told her there was no point ringing at the door. Nobody would be there. And anyway, we were happy here, on this bench. I could even hear a fountain flowing somewhere.

"Are you sure?" Louki said. "I can't hear anything . . ."

We were the couple who lived in the apartment, opposite. We had forgotten to switch off the light. And we had lost the key. The dog we saw a little while ago must be waiting for us. It had fallen asleep in our bedroom and would remain there waiting for us until the end of time.

Later on, we were walking northwards and, so as not to drift around too much, we had set ourselves a destination – place de la République – but we were not sure whether we were going the right way. No matter, we could always take the métro and go back to Argentine, if we got lost. Louki told me that she had often been in this neighbourhood, during her childhood. Her mother's friend, Guy Lavigne, had a garage in the area. Yes, near République. We stopped outside every garage, but it was never the right one. She could no longer find the way. The next time she visited this Guy Lavigne, in Auteuil, she would ask the exact address of his former garage before the man also vanished. It did not seem like very much, but it was important. Otherwise, you end up no longer having any reference point in life. She remembered that her mother and Guy Lavigne would take her, after Easter, on Saturdays, to the Foire du Trône. They would walk there along a large, endless boulevard similar to the one we were following. It may have been the same one. But we would be walking away from place de la République. On those Saturdays she used to walk with her mother and Guy Lavigne all the way to the edge of the Bois de Vincennes.

It was almost midnight, and it would be strange for both of us to find ourselves outside the gates to the zoo. We would be able to spot the elephants in the dusk. But over there, ahead of us, a brightly lit clearing unfolded in the midst of which a statue rose up. The place de la République. As we drew closer, we could hear the sound of music growing ever louder. An outdoor dance? I asked Louki whether it was Bastille Day. She knew no more than I did. For some time now, the days and the nights had been merging together for us. The music came from a café, almost on the corner of the boulevard and rue du Grand-Prieuré. A few customers were sitting outside.

It was too late to catch the last métro. Just past the café was a hotel with the door open. A bare bulb lit a very steep staircase with black wooden steps. The nightwatchman didn't even ask our names. He simply told us the number of a bedroom on the first floor. "Perhaps we could live here from now on," I said to Louki.

A single bed, but it wasn't too narrow for us. Neither curtains nor shutters on the window. We left it half-open because of the heat. Down below, the music had stopped, and we could hear roars of laughter. She whispered in my ear:

"You're right. We should always stay here."

I imagined that we were far from Paris, in a small Mediterranean port. Every morning, at the same time, we would walk along to the beaches. I have remembered the address of the hotel: 2 rue du Grand-Prieuré. Hôtel Hivernia. In the course of all the dreary years that followed, when I was occasionally asked for my address or my phone number, I would say: "You can just write to me at the Hivernia hotel, 2 rue du Grand-Prieuré. They'll forward it." I ought to go and collect all those letters that have been waiting for me for such a long time and have not been answered. You were right, we should have always stayed there.

I SAW GUY DE VERE AGAIN ONE LAST TIME, MANY YEARS later. In the sloping street that runs down towards the Odéon, a car draws up alongside me and I hear someone calling me by my former first name. Before turning round, I recognise the voice. He leans his head out of the lowered window of the car door. He smiles at me. He hasn't changed. Apart from the slightly shorter hair.

It was in July, at five o'clock in the afternoon. It was a warm day. We both sat on the bonnet of the car to talk. I didn't dare tell him that we were a few yards away from Le Condé and the door through which Louki always entered, the one on the shady side. But the door no longer existed. On this side, there was now a window in which crocodile-skin bags, boots and even a saddle and some riding-crops were displayed. Au Prince de Condé. Leatherware.

"So, Roland, what are you up to?"

It was still the same clear voice, the one that made the most abstruse texts accessible when he read them to us. I was touched that he should still remember me and the name I used at the time. So many people took part in the meetings in square Lowendal . . . Some only came once, out of curiosity, others came regularly. Louki was among this latter group. And so was I. Yet Guy de Vere was not seeking any disciples. He did not consider himself an intellectual guide and he refused to ·exert any kind of pressure on others. It was they who came to him, without his approaching them. Sometimes you imagined that he might have preferred to be on his own, daydreaming, but he could not refuse them anything, and especially not his help in enabling to see into themselves more clearly.

"And you, are you back in Paris?"

De Vere smiled and gazed at me with a quizzical look.

"You're still the same, Roland . . . You reply to one question with another question . . ."

He had not forgotten that either. He would often tease me about it. He told me that if I'd been a boxer, I would have been expert at the feint.

". . . I haven't lived in Paris for a long time, Roland . . . I live in Mexico now . . . I must give you my address . . ."

On the day that I had gone to find out if there really was ivy on the ground floor of the building where he used to live, I had asked the concierge for Guy de Vere's new address, if she happened to know it. She had told me simply: "Left without leaving an address." I told him about this pilgrimage to square Lowendal.

"You're incorrigible, Roland, with your business about ivy . . . I knew you when you were very young, didn't I? How old were you?"

"Twenty."

"Well, I reckon that at that age you were already setting off in search of lost ivy. Am I mistaken?"

His gaze lingered on me and misted over with a hint of sadness. We may have been thinking about the same thing, but I didn't dare utter the name of Louki.

"It's strange," I said to him. "At the time of our gatherings, I often used to come to this café which is no longer a café."

And I pointed out to him, a few yards from us, the leather-goods shop Au Prince de Condé.

"Yes, indeed," he said to me. "Paris has changed a good deal in recent years."

He frowned as he stared at me, as though he wished to recall a distant memory.

"Are you still working on neutral zones?"

The question was posed so abruptly that I did not realise what he was referring to straight away.

"It was rather interesting, your piece on neutral zones . . ."

My God, what a memory . . . I had forgotten that I had asked him to read this passage. One evening, after one of our meetings at his home, Louki and I had been the last to leave. I had asked him whether he might have a book that dealt with Eternal Recurrence. We were in his study and he glanced over at some of the shelves of his library. He had eventually found a book with a black and white jacket, *Nietzsche: Philosophy of the Eternal Recurrence of the Same*, which he had given me and which I read very carefully over the following days. The few typed pages to do with the neutral zones were in my coat pocket. I wanted to give them to him to obtain his opinion, but I hesitated. It was only just before leaving, on the landing, that I decided, on a sudden impulse, to hand him the envelope in which I had assembled these few pages – without saying a word to him.

"You also used to be very interested in astronomy," he said. "Particularly in dark matter . . ."

I could never have imagined that he would remember this. He had always been very solicitous of other people, in fact, but at the time we weren't aware of it.

"It's a pity," I told him, "that there isn't a gathering this evening at square Lowendal, as there used to be . . ."

He seemed surprised by my words. He smiled at me.

"Still your obsession with Eternal Recurrence . . ."

We were now walking back and forth along the pavement and, each time, our footsteps led us back to the leather-goods shop Au Prince de Condé.

"Do you remember the evening when there was a power cut at your home and you spoke to us in the dark?" I asked him.

"No."

"I'm going to confess something to you. That evening, I almost had a fit of the giggles."

"You should have let yourself go," he said to me in a reproach-ful tone of voice. "Laughter is infectious. We would all have laughed in the dark."

He looked at his watch.

"I'm going to have to leave you. I must pack my bags. I'm going back tomorrow. And I haven't even had time to ask you what you're doing at the moment."

He took out a diary from his inside pocket and tore out a page.

"I'm giving you my address in Mexico. You really should come and see me."

His voice suddenly took on an urgent tone, as though he wanted to take me with him and rescue me from myself. And from the present.

"And I continue with the gatherings there. Come. I'm counting on you."

He handed me the page.

"You also have my phone number. This time, let's not lose touch."

In the car, he leant his head once more out of the lowered window.

"Tell me . . . I often think of Louki . . . I still haven't understood why . . ."

He was moved. He, who always spoke without hesitation and in such a clear way, was now searching for words.

"It's ridiculous, what I'm saying to you . . . There's nothing to understand. When one really loves someone, one has to accept their mysterious side . . . And that's the reason one loves that person . . . Eh, Roland? . . ."

He sped off suddenly, probably so as to curb his emotions. And mine. He had time to say to me:

"See you very soon, Roland."

I was alone outside the leather-goods shop Au Prince de Condé. I pressed my forehead to the window to see whether any vestige remained of the café: a patch of wall, the door at the back that led to the telephone that hung from the wall, the spiral staircase that led to Mme Chadly's little apartment. Nothing. Everything was sleek and shiny and covered in an orange material. And it was like this everywhere in the area. At least, one was unlikely to meet any ghosts. The ghosts themselves were dead. Nothing to fear coming out of the Mabillon métro station. No more Pergola and no more Mocellini behind the window.

I walked with a light step as though I were arriving in a foreign city on a July evening. I began to whistle the tune of a Mexican song. But this falsely carefree manner did not last long. I walked past the railings of the Luxembourg and the tune of "Ay, Jalisco no te rajes" died on my lips. A poster was pasted to the trunk of one of the large trees whose foliage shelters us as far as the entrance to the gardens, up there, at Saint-Michel. "This tree is dangerous. It will be chopped down shortly. It will be replaced this winter." For a few seconds, I thought I was having a bad dream. I stood there, rooted to the spot, reading and re-reading this death sentence. A passer-by came and said to me, "Do you feel unwell, monsieur?", then he walked away, no doubt disappointed by my fixed stare. In this world in which I felt increasingly as if I were a survivor, they were also beheading the trees . . . I continued my walk, trying to think of something else, but it was difficult. I could not forget that poster and that tree that was sentenced to death. I wondered what the faces of the members of the court and the executioner looked like. I calmed down. To comfort myself, I imagined that Guy de Vere was walking beside me and in his soft voice kept repeating to me: ". . . Come now, Roland, it's a bad dream . . . one doesn't behead trees . . ."

I had passed the gate into the gardens and I was walking up the part of the boulevard that leads to Port-Royal. One evening, with Louki, we had walked home with a boy of our age whom we had met at Le Condé. He had pointed out to us, on our right, the École des Mines building, informing us in a sad voice, as though this admission were weighing on his mind, that he was a student at this school.

"Do you think I should stay there?"

I had sensed that he was expecting some encouragement from us to help him take the plunge. I had said to him: "No, my friend, don't stay there . . . Steer clear of it . . ."

He had turned towards Louki. He was waiting for her opinion as well. She had explained to him that ever since she'd been turned down by the Jules-Ferry lycée, she had distrusted schools. I think this succeeded in convincing him. The following day, at Le Condé, he told us that he was through with the École des Mines.

She and I would often take the same route to return to her hotel. It was a detour, but we were used to walking. Was it actually a detour? Not really, when I give it careful thought, more of a straight line, I reckon, towards the interior. At night, along avenue Denfert-Rochereau, it was as though we were in a provincial town, because of the silence and the doors of the religious hospices that followed one after the other. The other day, I walked along the street lined with plane trees and high walls that divides the Montparnasse cemetery in two. It was also the way to her hotel. I remember that she preferred to avoid it, and that was why we went via Denfert-Rochereau. But, more recently, we were no longer afraid of anything and we found that at night, beneath its canopy of leaves, this road that divides the cemetery did not lack a certain charm. No cars went by at that hour and we never encountered anyone there. I had forgotten to include it in the list of neutral zones. It was more of a frontier. When we reached the end, we were entering a land in which we were sheltered from everything. Last week, I wasn't walking there at night-time, but in the late afternoon. I hadn't gone back there since we had been there together or when I was on my way to join you at the hotel. For a moment, I imagined that I might find you beyond the cemetery. Over there, it would be the Eternal Recurrence. The same movements as before when taking your room key from reception. The same steep staircase. The same white door with its number: 11. The same waiting. And then the same lips, the same perfume and the same hair that comes cascading down.

I could still hear de Vere talking to me about Louki:

"I still haven't understood why . . . When one really loves someone, one has to accept their mysterious side . . ."

What was mysterious? I was convinced that we were alike, because we often had thought transmissions. We were on the same wavelength. Born in the same year and in the same month. Yet it would appear that there was a difference between us.

No, neither do I understand why . . . Especially when I remember the final weeks. The month of November, the days growing shorter, the autumn rains, none of that appeared to affect our spirits. We even made plans to travel. And then there was a joyful atmosphere at Le Condé. I no longer remember who it was that introduced that Bob Storms, who claimed to be a poet and a theatre director from Antwerp, to the regular customers. Adamov perhaps? Or Maurice Raphaël? He really made us laugh, this Bob Storms. He had a soft spot for Louki and for me. He wanted us both to spend the summer in his big house in Majorca. He evidently had no material worries. They said that he collected paintings . . . They say so many things . . . And then people disappear one day and you realise that you know nothing about them, not even their true identities.

Why should the massive figure of Bob Storms come back into my memory so strongly? In the saddest moments of life, there is often a discordant and subdued note, the face of a Flemish clown, a Bob Storms who passes by and who may have averted misfortune. He would stand at the bar, as though the wooden chairs were likely to collapse beneath his weight. He was so tall that one didn't notice his portliness. Always dressed in a sort of black velvet doublet the colour of which contrasted with his red beard and hair. And in a cape of the same colour. The evening when Louki and I had noticed him for the first time, he had walked over to our table and stared at us. Then he had smiled, and as he bent down towards us he had whispered: "*Compagnons des mauvais jours, je vous souhaite une bonne nuit.*" When he realised that I knew a great many lines of poetry, he had wanted to hold a competition with me. It would be for whoever had the last word. He would recite a line of verse to me, I had to recite another to him, and so on. It lasted a very long time. I deserved no credit for that. I was a sort of illiterate, without any general knowledge, but who had retained some lines of poetry, like those people who can play any piece of music on the piano without being able to sight-read. Bob Storms had this advantage over me: he also knew the entire repertory of English, Spanish and Flemish poetry. Standing at the bar, he let fly at me with a look of defiance:

I hear the Shadowy Horses, their long manes a-shake . . .
    or else:
Como todos los muertos que se olvidan
En un montón de perros apagados . . .
    or then:

De burgemeester heeft ons iets misdaan,

Wij leerden, door zijn schuld, het leven haten.

He exhausted me a little, but he was a very decent guy, much older than us. I should have liked him to tell me about his former lives. He always replied to my questions in an evasive manner. When he sensed that there was too much curiosity about him, his exuberance suddenly dissolved as though he had something to hide or he wished to put up a smokescreen. He wouldn't reply and eventually broke the silence by bursting out laughing.

There was a party at Bob Storms' place. He had invited us, Louki and me, along with the others: Annet, Don Carlos, Bowing, Zacharias, Mireille, La Houpa, Ali Cherif and the boy we had persuaded to leave the École des Mines. Other guests, but I didn't know them. He lived in an apartment on quai d'Anjou where the upstairs floor was a vast attic. He had us round there for a reading of a play he wanted to stage: "Hop Signor!" We both arrived before the others and I was struck by the candelabras that lit up the attic, the Sicilian and Flemish marionettes that hung from the beams, the mirrors and the Renaissance furniture. Bob Storms was wearing his black velvet doublet. A large bay window overlooked the Seine. In a protective gesture, he put his arms around Louki's and my shoulder and came out with his customary catch phrase:

Compagnons des mauvais jours
Je vous souhaite une bonne nuit.

Then he took an envelope from out of his pocket and handed it to me. He explained to us that it contained the keys of his house in Majorca and that we should go there as soon as possible. And stay there until September. He thought that we didn't look very well. What a strange party . . . The play only consisted of one act and the actors read through it fairly quickly. We were seated around them. From time to time, during the reading, at a sign from Bob Storms, we all had to shout out, as though we were part of a chorus: "Hop, Signor! . . ." Alcohol was passed around in generous measures. And other toxic substances. A buffet had been laid out in the middle of the large drawing room on the lower floor. It was Bob Storms himself who served drinks in goblets and crystal glasses. More and more people. At one moment, Storms introduced me to a man who was the same age as him, but much shorter, an American writer, a certain James Jones who he said was his "next-door neighbour on the landing". We ended up, Louki and I, not really knowing what we were doing among all these strange people. So many people whom we met when we were young, who will never know this and whom we'll never meet again.

We slipped away towards the exit. We felt sure that nobody had noticed our departure in this mêlée. But no sooner had we passed the drawing-room door than Bob Storms came to join us.

"So . . . Are you giving me the slip, kids?"

He was smiling as he usually did, a broad smile that with his beard and his height made him look like some character from the Renaissance or Grand Siècle, Rubens or Buckingham. And yet some anxiety showed in his eyes.

"You weren't too bored?"

"Not at all," I said to him. "'Hop Signor' was very good . . ."

He put both his arms around Louki's and my shoulders, just as he had done in the attic.

"Anyway, I hope to see you tomorrow . . ."

He drew us towards the door, still holding us by the shoulders.

"And be sure to set off to Majorca very soon to get some

fresh air . . . You need it . . . I've given you the keys to the house . . ."

On the landing, he looked at us both for a long time. Then he recited to me:

Le ciel est comme la tente déchirée d'un cirque pauvre.

Louki and I were going downstairs and he was leaning over the banister. He was waiting for me to quote a poem, in response to his, as was our usual way. But I couldn't come up with anything.

I have the feeling I'm mixing up the seasons. A few days after this party, I went to Auteuil with Louki. I think it was in summer, or else in winter, on one of those cold, clear mornings of sunshine and blue sky. She wanted to visit Guy Lavigne, the man who had been her mother's friend. I preferred to wait for her. We had arranged to meet "in one hour", on the corner of the street where the garage was. I believe we were intending to leave Paris because of the keys that Bob Storms had given us. Sometimes the heart sinks at the thought of things that might have been and that did not take place, but I tell myself that even today the house remains empty, waiting for us. That morning I felt happy. And light-hearted. And I experienced a degree of intoxication. The horizon lay far ahead of us, over there, towards infinity. A garage at the end of a quiet street. I regretted not having accompanied Louki to this Lavigne's place. Perhaps he was going to lend us a car so that we could drive south.

I saw her coming out through the small garage door. She waved to me, in just the same way as she had the other time, when I was waiting for them, her and Jeannette Gaul, in the summer, on the embankment. She is walking towards me with that same nonchalant gait, and it is as though she is slowing her pace, as though time no longer mattered. She takes my arm and we walk around the neighbourhood. This is where we shall live one day. What is more, we have always lived there. We walk along small streets, we cross a deserted roundabout. The village of Auteuil is quietly separating itself from Paris. These ochre and beige buildings could be on the Côte d'Azur and you wonder whether these walls are concealing a garden or the edge of a forest. We have reached the place de l'Église, in front of the métro station. And there, I can say it now that I have nothing more to lose: for the first time in my life I experienced what Eternal Recurrence was. Up until then, I did my best to read books on the subject, with the willingness of the self-educated. It was just before going down the stairs to Église d'Auteuil métro station. Why at this place? I have no idea and it is of no importance. I stood still for a moment and I held her arm tightly. There we were, together, in the same place, from time immemorial, and we had already done our walk through Auteuil over the course of thousands and thousands of other lives. No need to check my watch. I knew it was midday.

It happened in November. A Saturday. I had spent the morning and the afternoon at rue d'Argentine working on the neutral zones. I wanted to expand the four pages and write at least thirty more. It would snowball and I might achieve a hundred pages. I had a rendezvous with Louki at Le Condé at five o'clock. I had decided to leave rue d'Argentine in the next few days. I reckoned that the scars of my childhood and my adolescence were permanently healed and that, from now on, I no longer had any reason to remain hidden in a neutral zone.

I walked as far as the Étoile métro station. It was the line Louki and I had often taken to go to Guy de Vere's meetings, the line that we had followed on foot on the first occasion. As the train crossed the Seine, I noticed that there were a great number of walkers on the allée des Cygnes. Change at La Motte-Picquet-Grenelle.

I got off at Mabillon, and I glanced in the direction of La Pergola, as we always used to do. Mocellini was not sitting behind the window.

When I walked into Le Condé, the hands of the round clock on the wall at the back were pointing to five o'clock exactly. This was generally a slack period here. The tables were empty, apart from the one beside the door where Zacharias, Annet and Jean-Michel were sitting. All three of them gave me odd looks. They didn't say anything. Zacharias' and Annet's faces were pale, probably because of the light that shone from the window. They didn't answer when I greeted them. They stared at me with their strange expressions, as though I had done something wrong. Jean-Michel's lips were pursed, and I sensed that he wanted to talk to me. A fly settled on the back of Zacharias' hand and he dismissed it with a nervous flick. Then he picked up his glass and drained it in one. He stood up and walked over towards me. In a deadpan voice, he told me: "Louki. She threw herself out of the window."

I was afraid of going the wrong way. I went along Raspail and the street that cuts through the cemetery. When I reached the end, I no longer knew whether I should continue walking straight ahead or take rue Froidevaux. I took rue Froidevaux.

From that moment on, there has been an absence in my life, a white void that left me not merely with a feeling of emptiness, but which I could not look at directly. All this dazzling irradiance blinded me. And that is how it will be for evermore.

Much later, in Broussais Hospital, I was in a waiting room. A man of about fifty, with crew-cut grey hair and wearing a herring-bone pattern overcoat, was also waiting on the bench on the far side of the room. Apart from him and me, there was no-one there. The nurse came to tell me she was dead. The man drew closer to us, as though he were involved. I thought that it was Guy Lavigne, her mother's friend whom she had gone to see at his garage in Auteuil. I asked him:

"Are you Guy Lavigne?"

He shook his head.

"No. My name is Pierre Caisley."

We left Broussais together. It was dark. We walked side by side along rue Didot.

"And you, you're Roland, I suppose?"

How could he know my name? I was having difficulty walking. This whiteness, this radiant light ahead of me . . .

"Did she not leave a letter?" I asked him.

"No. Nothing."

It was he who told me everything. She was in the bedroom with a certain Jeannette Gaul who was known as Death's Head. But how did he know Jeannette's nickname? She had gone out onto the balcony. She had put one leg over the railing. The other girl had tried to restrain her by holding on to her dressing-gown. But it was too late. She had had time to utter a few words, as though she were talking to herself to boost her courage:

"That's it. Let yourself go."

PATRICK MODIANO was born in Paris in 1945. His first novel, *La Place de l'étoile*, was published in 1968 when he was just twenty-two and his works have now been translated into more than thirty languages around the world. He won the Austrian State Prize for European Literature in 2012, the 2010 Prix Mondial Cino Del Duca from the Institut de France for lifetime achievement, the 1978 Prix Goncourt for *Rue des boutiques obscures* and the 1972 Grand Prix du roman de l'Académie française for *Les boulevards de ceinture*. He was awarded the Nobel Prize in Literature in 2014.

EUAN CAMERON is an editor and translator. His translations include Patrick Modiano's novel *So You Don't Get Lost in the Neighbourhood*, works by Julien Green, Simone de Beauvoir, Paul Morand and Philippe Claudel, and biographies of Marcel Proust and Irène Némirovsky.

Patrick Modiano
PEDIGREE

Translated from the French by Mark Polizzotti

*"It's a book less on what I did than on what others,
mainly my parents, did to me"*

Taking in a vast gallery of extraordinary characters from Paris' post-war years, *Pedigree* is an autobiographical portrait of both post-war Paris and a tumultuous childhood – a childhood replete with the insecurity and sorrow that informed the œuvre of France's 2014 Nobel Laureate.

With his sometime-actress mother and shady businessman father almost entirely relinquishing their parental roles, the young Modiano spent his childhood being packed off to the care of others, or held at a safe distance in a decrepit boarding school, from where he ran away several times. His impecunious mother had "a heart of stone"; his womanising father once called the police when his son asked him for money, and later completely ceased all contact with him.

But for all his parents' indifference, it is the death of his younger brother when Modiano is eleven that cuts deepest, leaving a wound that can never be healed.

MACLEHOSE PRESS

www.maclehosepress.com

Subscribe to our monthly newsletter

Patrick Modiano
SO YOU DON'T GET LOST IN THE NEIGHBOURHOOD

Translated from the French by Euan Cameron

Jean Daragane, writer and recluse, has purposely built a life of seclusion away from the Parisian bustle. He doesn't see many people, he rarely goes out; he spends his life in a solitary world of his own making.

His peace is shattered however, one hot September afternoon, by a threatening phone call from a complete stranger, who claims to have found Daragane's old phone book and wants to question him about a particular name it contains. But when Daragane agrees to meet the mysterious Gilles Ottolini, he realises that, try as he might, he cannot place the name 'Guy Torstel' at all. Yet Ottolini is desperate for any information on this man . . .

Finding himself suddenly entangled in the lives of Ottolini and his beautiful, but fragile young associate, Daragane is drawn into the mystery of a decades-old murder that will drag him out of his lonely apartment and force him to confront the memory of a long-suppressed personal trauma.

MACLEHOSE PRESS

www.maclehosepress.com

Subscribe to our monthly newsletter

Patrick Modiano
THE BLACK NOTEBOOK

Translated from the French by Mark Polizzotti

"What would you say if I'd done something really serious? . . .
What would you say if I'd murdered somebody?"

A writer discovers a set of notes in his notebook and sets off on a journey through the Paris of his past, in search of the woman he loved forty years previously.

Along the left bank and through the Montparnasse district of Paris, Jean retraces the nocturnal footsteps he left decades earlier. Struggling to remember what brought him into contact with a gang that frequented the hotel Unic, his quest through seedy cafés and cheap hotels becomes an enquiry into a mysterious woman, Dannie, whom he once loved and who once tried to admit to a terrible crime.

As his memories overlap with the discovery of an old vice squad dossier, Jean reinvestigates the closed case of a crime where he could well be the last remaining witness.

MACLEHOSE PRESS

www.maclehosepress.com
Subscribe to our monthly newsletter